Contents

Lawfully Given

Elle E. Kay

Faith Writes Publishing
266 Saint Gabriels Rd
Benton, PA 17814

ISBN: 978-0-9994856-9-9

Books by Elle E. Kay

Faith Writes Publishing

Endless Mountain Series:
Shadowing Stella
Implicating Claudia
Chasing Sofie (coming soon)

The Lawkeeper Series:
Lawfully Held
A K-9 Lawkeeper Romance
Lawfully Taken
A Bounty Hunter Lawkeeper Romance
Lawfully Defended
A S.W.A.T. Lawkeeper Romance
Lawfully Given
A Christmas Lawkeeper Romance
Lawfully Promised
A Texas Ranger Lawkeeper Romance
(Releasing December 4, 2018)

Standalone novellas:
Holly's Noel
Painting the Sunset Sky (coming soon)

Introduction to The Lawkeeper Series

There's just something fascinating about a man wearing an emblem of authority. The way the light gleams off that shiny star on his badge makes us stare with respect. Couple that with a uniform hugging his body in just the right way, confidence, and mission to save and protect, it's no wonder we want to know what lies underneath.

Yes, what echoes deep inside those beating hearts is inspiring. Certainly appealing. Definitely enticing. Although those ripped muscles and strong shoulders can make a woman's heart skip a beat—or two—it takes a strong, confident person to choose to love someone who risks it all every day. Anyone willing to become part of a lawkeeper's world might have a story of their own to tell.

The undeniable charisma lawmen possess make all of us pause and take note. It's probably why there are so many movies and TV shows themed around the justice system. We're enthralled by their ability to save babies, help strangers, and rescue damsels in distress. We're captivated by their ability to protect and save, defend the innocent, risk their lives, and face danger without hesitation. Of course, we expect our heroes to stay solid when we're in a mess. We count on them for safety, security, and peace of mind. From yesterday to today, that truth remains constant.

Their valor inspires us, their integrity comforts, and their courage melts our hearts—irresistibly. But there's far more to them than their courageous efforts. How do they deal with the difficulties they face? Can they balance work and life? And how do they find time for love outside their life of service?

We want to invite you on a journey—come with us as we explore the complex lives of the men and women who serve and protect us every day. Join us in a fast-paced world of adventure. Walk into our tight-knit world of close friendships, extended family, and danger—as our super heroes navigate the most treacherous path of all—the road to love.

The Lawkeepers. Historical and modern-day super heroes; men and women of bravery and valor, taking love and law seriously. A multi-author series, sure to lock up your attention and take your heart into custody.

Visit The Lawkeepers on Facebook

Join our mailing list

The Lawkeepers is a multi-author series alternating between historical westerns and contemporary westerns featuring law enforcement heroes that span multiple agencies and generations. Join bestselling authors Jenna Brandt, Lorana Hoopes, Elle E. Kay, Patricia PacJac Caroll, Evangeline Kelly, Ginny Sterling and Barb Goss as they weave captivating, sweet, and inspirational stories of romance and suspense between the lawkeepers — and the women who love them.

The Lawkeepers is a world like no other; a world where lawkeepers and heroes are honored with unforgettable stories, characters, and love.

** Note: Each book in The Lawkeepers series is a standalone book, and part of a mini-series of sorts, and you can read them in any order.

This book is dedicated to Christ Jesus, who humbled Himself by coming down to earth as a babe and then giving His life to save mine.

Chapter One

"**W**ake-up!"

At the sound of the shrill voice, Sheriff Jack Garrison sat bolt upright and trained his Colt .45 on the petite woman who'd interrupted his nap.

"Put that gun away." She put both hands on her slim hips. "How did you do it?"

Jack growled low. "Do what?" He slid his weapon back into his holster.

"Convince my brother to send for me?" Her olive green eyes lit with the fire of her temper. Tendrils of her honey-colored hair fell loose around her face.

"Lady, I don't know what you're talking about, but you should come back when you've composed yourself."

"Calmed down?" She crossed the room and slammed both palms flat on his desk. "Would you be calm if your brother was missing and your only clue was a letter with a train ticket and a marriage proposition?"

"Missing?" He leaned back in his chair and put his feet up on his desk. "Who did you say was missing?"

"My brother. Calvin."

"Your brother probably ran off with a woman. If he doesn't return in a few days, come on back here and maybe I can help."

"He went missing from Philadelphia. The train ticket he left for me brought me here. So, where is he?"

"How do you know he didn't run off?"

"He would not have made arrangements for me to marry some sheriff in Podunk."

"Our town's name is Cimarron. Not Podunk." He grinned. "It's not unusual for a man to want a little alone time." Jack adjusted his hat to once again cover his eyes and tried to get comfortable again. "Now if you'll excuse me, I'd like to get some rest?"

"My brother is missing and I need your help to find him."

"You're not going to get it. At least not for the next few days. I have other obligations."

"Like sleeping the day away like a lazy dog?"

"Not that it's any of your business," he sat up straight, "but for your information, lady, I haven't been home in forty-eight hours. I had a run-in with some miscreants. They're sitting in cells over there." He pointed. "Would you care to join them?" Shoving his hat back on his head, he stood.

"I care not what the past two days brought you. Your prior obligations are none of my concern, but my brother's disappearance is my business and I expect you to drop everything, including your nap, to look for him." She slammed the note her brother had sent her onto the desk, and turned on her heel to walk out.

He spoke to her back. "Lady, you've gone mad."

"I have a name," she called over her shoulder.

"Care to share?"

She turned around. "Grace Belle."

"Miss Belle, why don't you go on home?"

"My home is in Philadelphia, and I will not return until Calvin is located." She crossed to the door and let it slam behind her.

Jack glanced down at the letter Grace had left on his desk. He should get home and sleep before he dealt with the silly woman from Philadelphia. Picking up the letter he read the careful script.

Grace,

My sincerest apologies for my sudden departure. I made arrangements for you to be wed in my absence.

I hope you will understand that my options were limited. Circumstances dictated that I depart Philadelphia posthaste. The danger was too great for you to accompany me.

Use the ticket I have provided to travel to Santa Fe. When you arrive, a stage coach will deliver you to Cimarron. Your betrothed is a man named Jack Garrison. He's the town sheriff. He will provide for you and protect you. When I am able, I will visit.

Trust me, Grace. This is for the best.

Be safe.

Calvin

The door banged open and Jack looked up, a smile slowly spread across his face. "Hello." He tipped his hat. "How can I help you today, Sarah?"

"I'm on the trail of Elmer Severil." She brushed away a stray hair that had escaped her bun. "Will Pinkerton wants me to cozy up to him and see if I can get any information from him on the stage coach robbery a few months back in Santa Fe."

"Will thinks Elmer was in on that?"

"He has a sneaking suspicion he hid the loot nearby and it's why he's back in Cimarron."

"Interesting theory." He stood and walked to the window, looking out over the dusty street. A glimpse of a debutante with honey-colored hair making her way down the road on foot made him laugh. There was no way that frivolous woman would survive in the New Mexico Territory on her own.

"Jack?"

"Sorry." He brushed off the distraction and concentrated on the lovely detective standing at his desk. "I'll check with Nate and Harry. They might know something."

"Perfect. Will they be in town soon?"

"Not that I know of, but I'll be heading out there. Something has come up."

"What's that?"

"Read this." He handed Sarah Jones the letter he'd read moments before she'd walked through the door.

"And I hoped we had a chance, sheriff."

"Sarah, I did not agree to marry that woman. I have no idea why her brother would claim I did."

"It's fine." She moved toward the door. "You shouldn't leave the lady waiting." Her tone was resigned, not angry.

Jack followed her out the door. "Wait! Sarah, don't go." The starch in her spine did not ease as she climbed atop her Appaloosa and rode away.

When he thought his day couldn't get any worse, he saw his supposed betrothed enter the St. James Hotel and saloon.

Grace felt a hand close around her arm. She swung around and instinctively slapped the man across his face.

Sheriff Garrison rubbed his face. "Was that necessary?"

"Maybe it will teach you some manners."

"I noticed you were heading into the St. James and I was hoping to speak with you about accommodations."

"Then speak."

"Despite its glamorous appearance, the St. James is notorious for hosting outlaws and prostitutes." We have a boarding house nearby that might suit you better."

"Is that so?"

"Would you care for an escort, so you won't be hassled on your way?"

"That will be unnecessary. I am sure to find it if you will point me in the correct direction."

"I would prefer to escort you there myself." He held his arm out for her to tuck her hand into.

She hesitated a moment before complying and letting herself be led away from the St. James. When he approached his stallion, she shook her head. "I have no intention of riding on that beast."

"His name is Bull and you'll need to ride if you want to move about in and around this town." He lifted her up and helped her to get settled on the stallion.

"I am not comfortable riding astride."

He mounted his horse in front of her. "That will have to change. I won't be able to find a saddle out here to suit your delicate preferences. I'll borrow a mare from Mr. Hayes' ranch tomorrow and you can practice, but for now, it's best if we get you settled at the boarding house." He looked back at her after Bull started moving.

"I thought you were unwilling to help me?"

"I need to find out who formed this marital arrangement on my behalf and why. So, I should be able to assist you in finding your brother in the process."

"You are honestly going to pretend you had nothing to do with bringing me here?"

"It's the truth. I am courting Sarah Jones. I hope to marry her."

"Then why bring me all the way out here under false pretenses?"

"I did no such thing."

"I have no intention of marrying you anyway."

"Why not?"

She held her tongue. The truth was, nobody was courting her and she would soon be labeled a spinster. Did she really expect Calvin to provide for her indefinitely? Her parents' fortune was passed to him not her. If she was unable or unwilling to find a husband, than it was time she considered gainful employment. Cimarron would not be the place to find work, but how would she return to Philadelphia with her dwindling funds? Calvin had not purchased her a return ticket. She needed to locate her brother promptly.

Arriving at the Rutherford's boarding house, Jack slowed the horse before dismounting and helping Grace down.

A plump woman ambled out of the house wrapping her shawl tighter around her shoulders. "Sheriff, it's a delight to see you. What brings you by?"

He glanced at Grace. "This young lady needs a safe place to stay. It seems she's my betrothed."

"I am not anyone's betrothed." Grace's tone was indignant.

Mrs. Rutherford's eyebrow shot up at the comment. The front door opened with a bang and a stout man came out.

"George. Nice to see you." Jack said. "Will you take exquisite care of Miss Belle for me?"

"She's Jack's fiancé." Mrs. Rutherford whispered. "Or not. Depending on which one of them you ask."

"Stay out of it, Eleanor." George grumbled. "Why don't you offer our new guest some dinner?"

Jack raked his hand through his hair. "I'll take care of any expenses."

Grace bristled, but didn't speak.

Mrs. Rutherford opened the front door. "You're more than welcome to join us for dinner before you head back out, sheriff." She placed a hand on Grace's shoulder and gently guiding her inside. Jack strolled toward the stables, whistling as he walked. He should be angrier about this whole mess. Whoever had set this up, was interfering with his life and he didn't have to stand for it.

On the other hand, he did need a wife, but Sarah would do fine. He took his time in the stables visiting the horses in the stalls and making sure everyone had water, since the stable boy was nowhere to be found.

As he moseyed back toward the house, he noticed the brilliance of the heavens. The colors streaking across the sky contrasted with the dark mountains creating a magnificent view. Almighty God was a fantastic artist for certain. He slowed his steps as he reached the staircase leading to the front porch. He hesitated at the door, not sure if he should knock or simply walk in. He settled on a compromise, he knocked once as he pushed the door open.

"What are you knocking for? Come in. Sit down. Dinner is ready. You took your sweet time out there." Mrs. Rutherford pulled the chair beside Grace out for Jack to sit down.

"Sorry about that. The stable boy wasn't around, so I watered the horses."

"Oh, Peter came down with something awful. He's in his room off the back of the stables. We're probably going to have to get the doctor out to see him."

"I'll let Doc Murphy know he's needed here when I get back to town."

"Much appreciated." George took a seat at the head of the table and said grace before continuing the conversation. "That young man is a hard worker. Deserves the best care."

"Of course," Jack replied.

Jack enjoyed his meal, but his gaze kept wondering over to the silent woman who seemed to be concentrating intently on the chicken and dumplings set before her. By the time she finished, there wasn't a speck of food left on her plate. She stood and helped Mrs. Rutherford clear the table.

"Are you going to marry her?" George asked when the women had left the room.

"I don't expect to."

"She's a quiet little thing."

"You wouldn't say that if you'd seen her when she stormed into my office earlier."

"Really?"

Jack stood and pushed his chair in. "She was quite the opposite."

Grace's cold stare met his. "Opposite of what?"

"Nothing. I should be going." Jack donned his hat from the hook by the door and turned back to his host. "Goodnight, George. I'll be back tomorrow with Doc Murphy."

"Thank you, sheriff."

Sleep wouldn't come. Grace tried to get comfortable under the weight of the quilt, but after tossing and turning for some time, she sat up and lit the lantern on the bedside table. She stood and fingered the Bible beside the lamp, but she didn't read it. Instead she stared down at the floorboards. They were clean, but scarred. The boarding house looked like it had been around for ages. She wondered if the Rutherfords were the original owners, but that wasn't the question haunting her this night. She had to find Calvin. She refused to believe he'd left Philadelphia willingly. There was more to the story and she intended to find out what it was.

If her brother wanted to marry her off, he'd have to find her another bachelor, because it was obvious the handsome sheriff intended to marry another. Not that she wanted to live out here in the middle of nowhere anyway. The mountains were beautiful, but there was nothing here. Where did people shop? Life in the New Mexico Territory was definitely not what she wanted for herself. She needed to find Calvin and return home. First thing in the morning, she would start her search.

The problem was, she had no idea where to begin. There were no leads to follow. There was nothing other than the note he'd left her and she'd left that with the sheriff. She would demand it back from him when he returned with the doctor. Something about the wording had been eating at her, maybe if she saw it again, it would come to her.

She walked to the window and looked out into the darkness of the night. Numerous stars shone along with a sliver of moon in the black sky. Hopefully, Calvin would know she was looking for him and wouldn't give up until he was home.

Grace crawled back into bed and picked up the worn leather Bible and hugged it to her chest, she breathed a prayer for Calvin's safety, set down the Bible and extinguished the lantern.

Jack returned to the boarding house with Doc Murphy in tow. As promised, he'd brought a mare along for Grace. Why he felt responsible for her, he wasn't sure. It wasn't like he'd actually agreed for a bride to be brought from back east. Despite his lack of involvement in her predicament, he felt he had to do something to rectify it. Finding out who'd arranged the whole thing would be a decent place to start.

"Doc, I've got some errands to run this morning, so do you mind letting Grace Belle know that this Palomino is a loaner for her to use until she returns to Philadelphia."

"Sure thing." The doctor stared over at the front porch. "Is that her?"

"Yes."

"Pretty little thing." Doc Murphy tipped his hat to the lady, hopped off his horse and led it toward the barn.

"Yes, she is." Jack swallowed the lump in his throat, following the other man and leading the mare to the stables.

Jack mounted his stallion.

"Why do you ride that beast?"

"He has quality blood lines and brings in considerable stud fees."

"You could keep him without having him as a regular rider."

"I suppose I could, but I only need one horse and he meets my needs."

"You sure you want to ride off without speaking to Grace?"

"I am."

"In that case, stay safe. Good day, sheriff."

"Good day."

Jack took a last look at the woman on the porch as he rode off. He raised his hand in greeting as Bull galloped off.

Doc was correct, she was a lovely lady, but that was no reason to mess up the satisfactory arrangement he had with Sarah. He needed to get his head on straight and stay away from Miss Belle.

He headed toward Santa Fe. If he pushed Bull hard, he would be there in less than two days. If he took his time, two and a half to three days was more realistic. Hopefully, he'd find some answers about Calvin Belle and this marriage sham.

Grace stood on the porch of the boarding house and greeted Dr. Murphy, but her gaze followed the sheriff as his horse carried him off. He'd promised to help her find Calvin, but now he was off to who knows where. Maybe he had bandits to chase down. It was just and proper for him to do his job. It would not do for her to wait around for the handsome sheriff to return. She would simply find Calvin without his assistance.

"Miss Belle?"

"My apologies. I was distracted."

"I was saying that there is a mare for you in the stables. The sheriff brought it from the Hayes' ranch this morning."

"That was considerate of him. Thank you for letting me know. After you've seen your patient, would you show me which horse it is, so I can introduce myself to her?"

"Certainly."

She paced the length of the porch as she waited to hear word on Peter's condition.

Her thoughts kept turning over in her head. There had to be somewhere logical that she could start her search. Then she remembered the hotel that the sheriff had steered her away from. Maybe someone in the saloon there would know something. It was a starting place anyway.

Since Dr. Murphy didn't know the mare's name, Grace decided to call her Buttercup. The Palomino was gentle, but slow. It took double the time to return to town as it had taken for her to be delivered to the boarding house. She wished she had access to a proper side-saddle. Riding astride was uncivilized.

When she arrived in front of the St. James Hotel, she tied her horse to a hitching post. A gentleman opened the door to the hotel for her and she smiled demurely as she made her way past him and toward the reception desk. Catcalls came floating toward her from the saloon where inebriated patrons were gathered. She lifted her chin and concentrated on the woman behind the desk.

"I was wondering if you might be able to assist me."

"What can I do for you? Do you need a room?"

"Not at the moment, but I may revisit the idea. I currently have a room at the boarding house."

The other woman lowered her voice in a conspiratorial whisper. "You should stay there. It is safer. There have been a number of shoot-outs in here."

"Oh, dear. Thank you for letting me know."

"Look up. See those bullet holes?"

Grace inspected the bullet ridden ceiling, cringing at the notion of outlaw gangs shooting up the fancy hotel.

"What is it I *can* help you with?"

"I am hoping to track down my brother. This is a photograph of him." She placed it on the desk. "Have you seen him?"

"He looks familiar. He may have been in here a week or so ago, but I am not positive."

"That is helpful. If you think of anything, would you let me know?"

"Yes. Of course."

Chapter Two

*J*ack finally arrived in Santa Fe. He'd ridden Bull harder than he should've, but arrived in less than two days. Now he hitched the stallion up to a post in front of the sheriff's office and hustled inside.

"Jack, it's great to see you." Nate came around the desk and slapped him on the back. "What brings you to Santa Fe? Telegraph machine broken?"

"No. It's working fine, but I thought it best I speak with you and Harry in person. I'm hoping you can help me."

"Of course. What is it?"

Jack handed Nate the note. "Read this."

"You sent for a mail-order bride?"

"That's the problem. I did not."

"Then what is this about?"

"I wish I knew."

"Aren't you courting Miss Jones?"

"I am." He scratched his head. "Or at least I was until she saw this note. She stormed out of my office and I haven't seen her since."

"You didn't follow her?"

"I had other concerns."

"Interesting."

"Why is that interesting?"

"If you were in love with Sarah, you would've followed her."

"What do you know? You've been married for a total of five minutes."

"Six months, but who's counting?"

Jack laughed.

"So, if you didn't agree to this marriage, who did? And who is this Calvin?"

"Another mystery. I've only met his sister."

"The bride? She's in Cimarron?"

"Yes. She is." He stuffed the note back in his pocket. "Miss Belle took the train to Santa Fe and then a stagecoach."

"Brave woman. I could interview some local troublemakers and see what I can find out."

"Would you? That would be great."

"In the meantime, I need to visit my father and see if he had anything to do with this."

"You think he would do that?"

"I wouldn't put it past him."

"Meet you back here after we interview witnesses?"

"Sure. Where's Addy?"

"She's supposed to be resting comfortably, but she's probably out trying to solve a murder. Harry loves having a detective around. I swear she's going to put me in an early grave."

Jack grinned. "She is perfect for you."

"Yes. She is." Nate beamed.

Jack took a deep breath to steady his nerves as he waited for his father to answer his knock.

"Jack, my boy." His father reached out a hand to shake his. "Come in."

He followed his father into the kitchen. "Coffee?" He turned to a pot resting on the cooker.

"I'd love some."

The two sat down at the table. "What brings you home, son?"

"Something strange, Pa."

His father raised an eyebrow.

"He put the note on the table for his father to read."

"You're getting married? To a mail-order bride."

"I didn't agree to marry anyone. I don't know who did so on my behalf. I was wondering if it was you."

"No. Of course not."

"You sure? You've been hounding me to get married for years."

"I wish I'd thought of it, but no."

"I'm glad it wasn't you."

"You should get married."

"You are aware that I've been courting Miss Jones."

"Stop courting and marry her."

"I'm not sure if she's the one. I like her, but I don't know if we're compatible."

"What about the mail-order bride?"

"She's not an actual mail-order bride. She didn't agree to this either. Grace only came to town to find her brother. Her concern is for her brother's safety."

"Is he in danger?"

"She seems to think so. I have Nate and Harry looking into it." He looked into his cup. "When I get back, I'll spend some time in the saloon and see what chatter I can pick-up there."

"I hope you learn something." His father reached across the table and patted the top of his hand. "Do you want to stay for Thanksgiving, son. We could have a nice family meal."

"Without Edward?"

"I haven't seen your brother in months."

"You wouldn't tell me if you had."

"I can't have you arrest your own brother."

"You can't harbor a fugitive, Pa."

"He's not here, Jack. How about Thanksgiving dinner?"

"I wish I could, but you know I can't stay. I need to get back to town in case anything goes awry. Why don't you take the stage coach to Cimarron and have Thanksgiving dinner at my place."

"I wouldn't want to impose."

"It wouldn't be an imposition. I'd like for you to come."

"Will you cook?"

"I'll ask Sarah. Or Grace."

"You'd better figure out which one before you start inviting people to dinner."

"True." He set down his mug. "Do you think it would be weird to ask both of them?"

"Yes." His father grinned. "But somehow, I think you'll pull it off."

Back at the boarding house, Grace helped Mrs. Rutherford serve dinner. "You are a guest. You should be resting."

Grace set the dish of roasted potatoes on the table. "Nonsense. It does me good to help out."

"Well, if you want to help, I won't stop you."

"Do you think Sheriff Garrison will return?" She followed Mrs. Rutherford back to the kitchen.

"I imagine so, but not for several days."

"Oh?"

"Dr. Murphy said he rode out to Santa Fe this morning." She handed Grace a butter dish.

"Is that so?"

"Yes. He's got kin out that way. Friends too." Mrs. Rutherford set a tray of chicken out on the table.

"Is he visiting them for Thanksgiving?"

"He didn't say, but I doubt he would."

"Why is that?"

"He would want to be in town in case anyone got too rowdy. We don't have a deputy sheriff. Sheriff Garrison is our only lawman."

"That must be difficult for him."

"He doesn't seem to mind. Care to ring the dinner bell? It'll bring the men to the table."

Grace grinned. "Definitely." She hadn't used a dinner bell before. Mrs. Rutherford explained that it was a cow bell, but she used it to call everyone to dinner. It was easier than tracking down the guests individually.

Soon everyone joined them around the table. She was surprised to see the latest guest was a woman a few years her junior.

"So, Miss Belle, what brings you to Cimarron?" Sarah asked once they'd been introduced.

"You may call me Grace." She set her fork down. "I received a train ticket from my brother, so I was hoping he would be in town."

"And did you locate him?" Sarah sat with perfect posture, raising an eyebrow.

"Unfortunately, I did not."

"Then will you be headed back to Philadelphia?"

"How do you know where I am from?"

"Sheriff Garrison showed me your letter."

Grace's cheeks grew warm. "I was not aware he'd shared that with anyone."

"That color agrees with you. You should blush more often. You're too pale."

"Sarah! That is completely inappropriate."

"Mrs. Rutherford, I'm simply having fun."

"Mind your manners."

"My apologies." Sarah looked down at her plate and then gave Grace a conspiratorial smile. "Want to take a walk after dinner?"

Grace wasn't ready to spend time with the other woman, but didn't know how to bow out gracefully. "That might be nice." She turned to face Dr. Murphy. "How is Peter?"

"His fever broke about an hour ago. We'll need to keep a watch on him, but I think he will pull through."

"That is wonderful news."

After helping clean up from dinner, Grace joined Sarah out on the porch. Sarah led the way down the steps and onto the dusty road. The sun was beginning to descend.

Sarah stared up at the sky. "It will be dark again tonight. The moon was barely visible last night."

"I noticed that."

Slowing her steps, Sarah looked Grace in the eyes. "Did Jack mention that we were seeing each other?"

"Yes, he did."

"Honestly?"

"He did."

"Why did he bring you here?"

"I believe him when he says he was unaware of the arrangement my brother made." Grace sighed. "I believed he was lying at first, but he has me convinced now."

"Then how did your brother come to know that Jack was looking for a wife?"

"I wish I knew. Such information would get me one step closer to finding Calvin."

"We should get back before darkness descends." Sarah turned back toward the boarding house. "I usually stay here when I'm in town. I was stuck at the St. James yesterday because my work required it, but I am grateful to be back here with the Rutherfords."

"What do you do?"

"I work for the Pinkerton Agency as a detective."

"Really?"

"Yes. I'm on an assignment now."

"I heard they had lady detectives, but I never met one before."

"What do you do?"

"This and that. I'm not employed, but I keep the household running smoothly for my brother. It may be time to consider some form of employment since Calvin is missing and the funds he last gave me are dwindling."

"What would you do?"

"I wish I knew."

Jack checked in with Nate before riding back to Cimarron. One of the men he'd interviewed had a run-in with the Slocum Gang and had seen Edward Garrison in town. The bandit had suggested a connection to the Philadelphia man and his sister, but wasn't able to demonstrate an actual link. Jack tucked the idea away, wondering if it was possible his brother was somehow behind these current circumstances.

He stopped along the creek and made ready his camp for the night. The aroma of wet sage surrounded him as an extravagant lightning show lit the sky. Jack started a fire for warmth, certain temperatures had dipped below freezing. Rolling out his bedroll, he allowed himself a few hours of sleep.

Morning found him stalking a rabbit across the frost coated landscape. The poor creature had the misfortune of straying too close to camp, and although he wasn't fond of hunting, he was glad of the hot meal.

When Jack finally rode up to the boarding house, he was surprised to find Sarah and Grace sitting on the front porch swing together chatting like childhood friends.

"Hello, ladies."

"Did you find any news on Calvin?"

"I'm afraid not."

"How was your trip?" Sarah asked.

"Sorry. I should have told you I was leaving."

"No. It's my fault. I'm sure you would have if I hadn't walked out of your office without giving you a chance to explain. Grace has since clarified the situation for me."

Grace felt a surge of jealousy, but tamped it down. There was no reason to be jealous. She didn't even know the sheriff and certainly had no claim on him. "I'll leave you two to catch up."

"I actually want to speak to both of you."

"Oh?"

"I was wondering if you might both be my guests for Thanksgiving dinner."

"I would not wish to impose. I will have dinner here at the boarding house. Mrs. Rutherford will appreciate the help."

"My father is coming and I could use the assistance."

Sarah grinned. "Let's help him, Grace. It will be fun. Besides with both of us tongues will be sure to wag. I love causing gossip."

Jack laughed. "You have a strange sense of humor, Miss Jones."

"Thank you." Sarah giggled.

"I suppose I will join you," Grace said.

"Marvelous. We'll have fun. You'll see." Sarah squeezed Grace's hand.

Grace wasn't sure how to broach the subject gracefully, so she asked outright. "Sheriff, may I have my brother's missive returned?"

"It's evidence in his disappearance, Miss Belle."

"You know what it says, so it cannot provide you with additional assistance, but I would find it a comfort to have it in my possession."

He pulled it from his pocket and handed it to her. "Thank you." She was surprised he had it with him, but said nothing of it.

"I thought Sarah was supposed to be here. And where is your father?" Grace moved around the tiny kitchen trying to put together dinner.

"Sarah *is* supposed to be present. The Pinkertons may have called her away."

"And your father?"

"He should've been here by now. The stage coach was supposed to arrive an hour ago."

"You should go find him. I'll take care of this."

"Are you sure?"

"I am not comfortable being alone with a man. As Sarah said, tongues will wag."

"Yes, they will. So, let them."

"That is not my style, Sheriff Garrison."

"No. I wouldn't imagine it was." He grinned. "What is your style, Miss Belle?"

"I'm old-fashioned. I think a woman should be courted and treated with respect, not given to be married to a man she never met by a brother whose gone missing."

"Is that how you see it?"

"Why would he do that?"

"I'm guessing he got into some kind of trouble, Grace."

"Grace. Not Miss Belle?"

"Do you mind my calling you by your given name?"

"I should, but I do not."

"Grace, I don't know your brother, but you speak highly of him. Somehow, he must've been convinced he was doing the honorable thing."

"By sending me off to marry a man set to wed another? How will I find him?"

"I wish I could answer that. I traveled to Santa Fe and asked the lawkeepers there for assistance. They've found a lead, but it's thin."

She brushed a tear away. "Tell me. What did they find?"

"It isn't enough to go on yet."

"I need to know." Grace looked up into his kindly hazel eyes. The next thing she knew he was pulling her close as if to comfort her, but it was not comfort that she felt in his arms. For a moment, she dared to wish he was unattached and that he might be interested in a woman like her. The idea was silly. She was no strong western woman. Her talents did not involve cooking, cleaning, canning, and milking goats. It was all she could do to put together a passable meal this day without Sarah's promised assistance.

"Will you be all right?" With his thumb, he brushed away a tear from her cheek that she hadn't realized was there. Pulling away, she leaned back inside the circle of his arms. There was no advantage to allowing herself the comfort of a man she could never have.

A loud bang on the door startled her and she jumped. He released her, and went to answer the knock.

Jack opened the front door to greet the fellow who'd been banging on it. "Sheriff, come quick."

"What's going on?" Jack reached up to grab his hat off the stand.

"An unconscious man outside the saloon."

"Go get Doc Murphy."

"He's out at the boarding house for dinner."

"Go after him. Bar fight?" He took a step inside and motioned for the messenger to do the same.

"Don't know. He was lying on the ground and I tripped over him."

"Was he alive?"

"I don't know." He bounced nervously from one foot to the other and back again.

"You didn't check for a pulse?" Jack raked his fingers through his hair.

The young man shook his head.

"If he's still camping outside of town, alert the traveling preacher on your way to fetch Doc Murphy, would you?"

"Of course."

"I'll head right over to the saloon," Jack said.

"Hurry."

"I will." Once he galloped away, Jack headed back into the kitchen.

"I assume you heard that?"

Her face reddened. "It would be hard not to eavesdrop in this place."

"I'm going to have to go take care of this. Do you want to wait here or join me in town? It's not glamorous, but you can see me at work."

"It's probably better if I go back to the boarding house, but I could join you for a moment to determine if the unconscious man is Calvin."

"I hadn't even considered that. Come on then."

"Let me put this food away," Grace said.

"No time. I'll take care of it when I get back."

Jack stood over the man who'd been dragged into the saloon and glanced down at Grace. "It's definitely not your brother."

"No. Thank the Lord." Grace closed her eyes a moment before looking up at Jack. "Do you have any idea who he might be?"

"It's *my* brother."

"Your brother?" She placed her hand on his arm. "My deepest sympathies. Were the two of you close?"

"I haven't seen him in five years. I chose the life of a lawkeeper and he chose the life of an outlaw. Our lifestyles didn't mesh."

"That must have proved difficult." She lowered her eyes to the ground.

He stormed out the front door. Moments later, her soft footfalls came up behind him. When he turned toward her, she wrapped her arms around his waist and leaned back so she could look into his eyes. "Are you going to be all right?"

He met her gaze. "Fine." A muscle twitched in his jaw. Any other time he would be tempted to take advantage of her inappropriate affectionate display. He might've even let himself kiss her, yet as much as he wanted to lose himself in her embrace and forget about Edward, it wouldn't be proper. He extricated himself from her arms and moved a safe distance away. "I think we might have a piece of the puzzle. I'm willing to bet my brother made that arrangement with your brother. Edward being in town while all this is going down can't be a coincidence. Now we need to find Calvin and ask him if he killed Edward."

"My brother would not harm a soul. He is as gentle as a butterflies wings."

"Maybe he would if it was to protect someone he loved. Someone like you."

"Once you locate him, you can ask him."

"There is nothing more for me to do here. Let's go back to my place and see if my father shows up. If he does, I can tell him about Edward. If not, I'll telegram Santa Fe and let him know."

She gasped. "You cannot send a telegram to inform him of the death of his child. It would be cruel."

"I'll send the telegram to a friend who will go to the house."

"I should return to the boarding house and leave you alone with your grief."

"Please stay." He should send her away, but the desire to have her near was intense. "It's Thanksgiving. I'd like the company. After we eat, I'll ride with you back to the boarding house."

"Yes. That would be acceptable."

He laughed. "Your speech is odd."

"How so?"

"Formal. Nobody in the west is as stiff."

"Are you mocking my speech?"

"No. I quite like your prim and proper manner."

He knew he shouldn't be teasing her at what should be a solemn moment, but he was having difficulty grasping the fact that Edward was dead. It didn't seem real and he wasn't prepared to accept it.

Chapter Three

*A*fter Jack asked the blessing on the food, they ate in silence. As they were finishing up, another knock came on the front door. Grace stood and began clearing the table while Jack answered it. She heard Sarah and another male voice. A moment later Sarah appeared in the kitchen.

"I brought Mr. Garrison. He and I both got held up on the stagecoach earlier. I'm sorry I wasn't here to help prepare the meal."

"Has he told his father?"

"Told him what?"

"His brother is dead."

Sarah stumbled backward. "Edward?"

"Yes." Grace put her arm around the other woman. "Did you know him?"

"He was my current case. I'm investigating him."

"Does Jack know that?"

"No. My boss thought it was best that I not mention it to him. He was afraid it would compromise the case. It's been killing me to keep it from him."

Sarah pulled away and began pacing.

"Jack thinks his brother might have been behind the fake arranged marriage."

"I wouldn't put it past him." She smiled. "He was quite the charmer, but he had a dark side."

"I should head back to the boarding house, so that I can give Jack and his father some privacy."

"I'll join you."

"Let's fix you a plate first. You must be starved."

"I am."

Grace rushed about heating up food and fixing plates. She gave Sarah her meal and took the other to Jack for his father. Then she went back in to sit with Sarah. "Do you really think Edward and my brother knew each other? It seems so far-fetched that my brother would have anything to do with an outlaw."

"One thing I've learned in my line of work is that you never truly know anyone. People I would assume are incapable of bad deeds are secretly some of the worst miscreants."

"How do you do it?"

"Do what?" Sarah asked between bites.

"Try to fit in with the worst of humanity in order to fight them."

"It wasn't easy at first, but I got used to it." She sighed. "Most of my work isn't quite so glamorous. Sometimes I'm nothing more than a hired guard. Other times I'm sitting at a desk examining papers. It's rare that I get to work on a case that offers the unique challenges that Edward's case has."

"What were the unique challenges?"

"I had to get close to him."

As the words came out of her mouth, Jack walked into the room. "Get close to him? Him who?" The sharp edge to his words made it clear he already knew.

"I'm sorry. Will didn't want me to tell you."

"I'll clean this up later. Maybe you should ride with Grace and I'll escort the three of you to the boarding house."

Sarah frowned. "I'm sure your father would make a fine escort for Grace."

"There is a killer on the loose. Nobody leaves alone."

"Why do you think it was murder?" Grace asked.

"Dear, sweet Grace. I know I mentioned that your brother is my prime suspect. Surely you understood then that it was murder. Didn't you see the marks around his neck? Edward was strangled. He did not die of natural causes."

"Tomorrow we'll search for Calvin. In the meantime, it's best that we head to the boarding house."

A soft knock on the bedroom door got Grace's attention. She gasped as her feet touched the cold floor. She opened the door a sliver to see who was out there.

"May I come in?" Sarah hiccupped.

"Yes. Come in." She ushered the other woman to the chair and sat down on the edge of the bed. "Are you tipsy?"

"I had some whiskey. Did you see how angry Jack was? He couldn't even look at me."

"I am sympathetic, Sarah."

"Are you?" Sarah pulled her knees up to her chest and buried her face in them. "I've seen how the two of you look at each other."

"Nonsense." Grace walked over to the other woman and knelt in front of her. "He cares for you. The sheriff is kind to me because he feels sorry for me. It does not change how he feels about you."

Sarah sniffled. "Jack Garrison never felt more than a passing attraction for me. He latched on to me because I was the only single woman who came through town not working as a courtesan."

"You cannot be serious?"

"I am."

"Are there that many prostitutes in town?"

"No. There are that few women."

"Oh."

"The few women around here are married."

"I see."

"So, if you're interested in sticking around, there is no shortage of eligible bachelors. It's part of what is keeping me here. The Pinkertons can send me anywhere, but they've been indulging my desire to get to know Jack."

"Then you shouldn't abandon hope so easily." Grace stood.

"Don't you comprehend what's transpired?"

"I fear I do not."

"He looked at me like I was lower than a worm. He will not forgive my transgression. I should've told him about my case involving his brother."

"You love him, don't you?" Grace slid to the floor and leaned against the bed, closing her eyes.

Sarah took a deep breath and sighed. "Love is a peculiar thing. I'm not sure I love him, but I'm fond of him and could grow to love him."

"You don't believe instantaneous love is possible?"

"No. Love must develop over time."

"I wonder if it isn't a little of both."

"You may be confusing love with attraction. It's more important that a couple is compatible than that they love each other, don't you think?"

"I'm not certain about that. If I'd subscribed to that philosophy, I may have avoided becoming an old maid."

"Who told you you're an old maid?"

"My brother. Jokingly, of course, but it is true, nonetheless."

"How old are you?"

"Twenty-eight."

"You *are* old." Sarah's musical laugh mocked her. "You should marry Jack."

"You are mad."

"He won't have me now, but he still needs a wife."

"You've had too much strong drink and it's addled your mind. Get some sleep. You can reconcile with Sheriff Garrison on the morrow."

Jack sat beside his father in front of the fire at the boarding house. He struggled to restrain his temper. His father was in mourning and it wasn't the time for him to lose control. He'd lied to him about having seen Edward in the last several months, but Edward was his son. He'd protected him out of love not to thwart Jack's duties. If he'd arrested Edward, he would be safe in a cell instead of lying dead on the slab in Doc Murphy's makeshift mortuary. They would have to bury him. What did you say at the funeral of a brother you'd once loved, but had come to despise?

The knots in his stomach grew tighter when his father spoke. "It's come to this. I should've known it would."

"He chose his path."

"I don't think he chose to die in the road outside a saloon."

"Do you have any idea what he was doing here, Pa?"

"I wish I did. He came by a few weeks back asking about you. Wanted to know about whether you had settled down yet."

A muscle twitched in Jack's jaw as he tried to rein-in his emotions. "And you told him everything."

"I didn't mention Sarah."

"Which put Grace in danger."

"How could I have known that?" His father looked wounded.

"I'm sorry, Pa. I know this isn't your fault."

"I have to bury my firstborn son."

"I know."

A tear slid down his father's cheek. "I hoped and prayed he would turn from his wicked ways."

"A worthwhile dream." He rested his hand on his father's shoulder.

Grace settled Sarah in her bed and then made her way down the creaky stairs trying to do so as quietly as possible. It was no use though, two heads turned toward her as she reached the foot of the stairs. The sheriff was sitting by the fire with his father.

"I'm going to head up to bed." Mr. Garrison stood.

"Goodnight, Pa."

"Try to get some sleep, son." He tipped his hat to Grace.

"Are you going to hold that post up all night, Miss Belle?"

"What?"

"You're leaning against the baluster as if you're the only thing holding it upright. Evidently, you weren't expecting me to be down here. His eyes wandered down the length of her dressing-gown."

"Obviously."

"Why don't you come sit with me?"

"I came down to make a warm drink," Grace said.

"Then why don't we go in the kitchen and have some tea?"

She walked toward the kitchen and he followed closely behind her.

Ten minutes later they settled down in front of the fire with their cups of tea.

"Do you think you can forgive Sarah?"

"Yes."

"Glad to hear it. She was rather upset when she came to my room thinking that she'd ruined everything with you."

"She has."

"I thought you said you could forgive her?"

"Forgiveness is one thing. Trust is another." He shook his head. "I will never trust her."

"Doesn't love matter?" She lifted her face so she could see his eyes. "Don't you love her?"

"Sarah and I were not courting because we loved each other. We were seeing each other because I needed a wife and she desired a husband. It was a simple matter of convenience. We liked each other fine, but marriage is not about love."

She leaned back in the chair and closed her eyes. When she opened them again she found him staring. "What is it?"

"You believe in love? You came all the way out here for a marriage of convenience, but you believe in love."

"I came out here to find my brother. If all else fails and I cannot find him, I suppose I will find employment before I marry for the sake of having a provider."

"A husband is more than a provider, Miss Belle. A husband is a protector and a companion."

"I could find all that in a loyal dog."

He chuckled. "Yes, I suppose you could."

"You're holding out for love?"

"I am."

Jack stared at the spot where Edward's body would be buried in a few short minutes. A simple pine casket held the shell that had once been his brother. There were some great memories that he didn't wish to bury with him, but his pain at not being able to lead Edward to the Lord overwhelmed him and wouldn't allow reflection on happier times. His father stood beside him allowing silent tears to fall, but his own tears were bottled up tightly.

There would be no preacher, as the circuit rider had moved on to another town. A delicate touch on his shoulder caused him to glance at the woman standing slightly behind him. He took a step forward to escape her touch. Now wasn't the time for making amends. His heart was in tatters and Sarah's involvement was too fresh in his mind. Had she told him Edward was in town and involved in something bad, maybe he could've stopped this from happening.

If he hadn't died here, it would've been in some unknown town doing business for some other unsavory characters. It was the life Edward chose, a life of crime. While his brother's choices were not Sarah's fault, he wasn't ready to make the distinction. The anger was too fresh.

This was far from his first burial, but somehow it was different. When his mother had passed, her life had meant something, he knew she would spend eternity with her Savior. Most other deaths, hadn't prompted him to consider the eternal implications, as he did now. In this instance, his anger ate him from the inside out. He was angry with Sarah, with his father, with his brother, but mostly with himself. He should've done more.

Grace sat on the porch and picked at her nails. Pouring over Calvin's letter the night before, she discovered what had been bothering her about it. The words 'trust me,' were out of character for him. He warned her repeatedly never to trust a soul who used those words. He likely used them to warn her not to come, but she had missed the meaning. The knots in her stomach seemed to wind tighter. His message would not have kept her from coming. If it was a warning, it only proved he was in danger and needed assistance.

She had no clue how to go about finding her brother. Her only hope was that Sarah might be able to help her. If Jack was correct and Calvin had made the marriage arrangement with his brother, then Sarah might have some lead that Grace could follow to find him.

She stood and made her way back inside to find Sarah. She found her in the kitchen with Mrs. Rutherford. "Sarah, I have a favor to ask."

"Want to walk and talk? I need to stretch my legs for a bit."

"All right."

When they had walked for a few minutes, Grace brought up her plan. "I'd like to follow whatever leads you found on your case against Edward."

"Why would you do that? Are you looking to become a Pinkerton agent?"

"No. Nothing like that. I'm hoping that you can show me how to investigate, so that I can find my brother. Your case may very well be the jumping off point I need to find Calvin."

"I don't know how much I can help, but I'm happy to be of service. Let's get to work."

When they got back inside, Sarah got her notebook and the two of them sat by the fire pouring over her notes for hours.

Sarah pointed at a page. "We might be able to start here."

Grace read the section and agreed. "Looks promising."

They hurried out to the barn and saddled their horses for the ride back into town. "Stay close to me and don't go off on your own."

When they arrived at the St. James, Sarah brought Grace in by the rear entrance and ushered her up the stairs to a room used by the courtesans. "We should be able to hear most of the conversation from here."

"Will we get in trouble?"

"Not unless we're caught eavesdropping."

Grace peered through the hole and saw a group of men around a table. They had cards out on the table, but they weren't looking at them. The discussion was a heated one. This was some sort of meeting just as Sarah had noted in her case file. They listened intently until finally something caught Grace's attention. "Did you hear that?" she whispered.

"About a captive? Yes." She put her finger to her lips.

Twenty minutes later they had a location where they were keeping their captive. As they made their way down the stairs, Grace finally allowed herself to hope. "Do you think it's possible they're holding Calvin?"

"Don't get your hopes up." Sarah smiled. "Whoever their holding got Little John's daughter pregnant. If that was Calvin, he's made himself a formidable enemy."

They left their horses in a secluded spot and proceeded on foot. It wasn't much farther to reach the shack on the back of the Frazer Ranch. If Calvin was here, they'd be able to alert the sheriff and rescue him, but they needed to confirm that it was him first.

Sarah stood watch while Grace crept close to the shack to peer through the wooden slats. Calvin was tied to a chair, dried blood covered his face. A gasp escaped Grace's throat, and the man behind Calvin cocked his revolver and pointed it at Grace.

Sarah shouted, "Grace, run!"

Grace turned toward the sound and saw Sarah fighting off an attacker. A gunshot rang out from inside the shack and Grace froze. She watched as Sarah kicked the bandit hard and ran off in the direction of the horses.

The outlaw grinned and meandered toward Grace. "Little John will be pleased. Glad you could come all this way. You may even be worth the price of the ticket." He dragged her with him into the shack and tied her to a chair.

When darkness fell, the bandits dozed.

"What are you doing here, Grace?" Calvin whispered.

"You sent for me." Grace wanted to shout, but kept her voice low, so as not to disturb the miscreants.

"I expected you would know the missive was sent under duress. I said 'trust me' near the end. I've warned you never to trust a man who says trust me. They wanted you here, so they could hurt you to cause me pain."

"Why are they doing this?"

One of the bandits stirred and Calvin fell silent for a time.

Grace was sure help was on the way, but the outlaws witnessed Sarah's escape, so they would be planning a move. Grace prayed that the sheriff would arrive on time.

"Sarah escaped. She'll be getting the sheriff."

"We don't have much time. They've been waiting for Little John Slocum to arrive, so he can have the pleasure of torturing and killing me himself."

"Did you really impregnate his daughter?"

"No." He sighed. "Maria came to me for help. She was my student at the University and we instantly hit it off. When she discovered her pregnancy, she panicked. Not knowing where else to turn, she came to me and begged me to marry her, so her child would have a chance at legitimacy."

"And you agreed to this?"

"I did, but something went terribly wrong. I was accosted on my way home from work. The men who grabbed me accused me of violating Maria and dragged me off to the territories."

"Is she here?"

"I haven't seen her since the day she told me she was with child."

"Do you think she is safe?"

He nodded. "Her father probably locked her away somewhere."

"Let's hope Jack gets here before we're moved. Or murdered."

"I wouldn't count on it. Last I heard, Little John was only about three hours away and you've been here nearly that long."

"He might stop off somewhere first."

"Maybe." Calvin's voice was resigned.

"It's wonderful to see you alive."

"I won't say the same. I wish you'd stayed away. I could not stand seeing harm come to you, I would rather they put a bullet in my head."

"Don't say that. You had to know I would come to look for you."

"I did, but hoped against it."

"Who is this Sarah you said got away?"

"She's a detective with the Pinkerton agency. Sheriff Garrison has been courting her."

"Interesting."

"How so?"

"I overheard Edward Garrison talking to Little John and he said that his sheriff brother had no romantic entanglements and was looking for a simple marriage of convenience. That's how they came up with the idea of sending for you. I knew you wouldn't agree to the marriage, but I was afraid you would come and put yourself in danger."

"You think you know me so well."

The bandits stirred.

Chapter Four

"How did you let this happen?" Jack raked his fingers through his hair.

"How is this my fault?" Sarah put a hand on her hip.

The muscles in Jack's jaw tensed. "You seriously don't know?"

"She came to me for help. I helped."

"You took a well-to-do lady from Philadelphia's society and turned her loose near an outlaw hideout in the New Mexico Territory without any backup. Then you allowed her to get caught." He turned from her and stormed out of his office.

As he saddled his horse, she came up to him again. "I was trying to help."

"You should've come to me first." He mounted his stallion.

"You weren't exactly talking to me." She strained her neck to look up at him. "You wouldn't even look at me."

"True, but can you blame me?" He turned the horse around and then looked over his shoulder at her. "You betrayed my trust."

He knew Sarah would mount her Appaloosa and hurry to catch him, but wished she would stay out of his way. She'd done enough.

When Sarah caught up to him her mare fell into step beside Bull. "I know the timing is poor, but I want to talk to you about Grace."

"What about her?"

"You have my blessing if you want to pursue her."

"And why would I want to do that?"

"Jack, there is no need to pretend. I've seen how you look at her and how protective you've become of her."

"It's my job to protect strangers who come to this town."

"And you're taking that job to the extreme in this case."

He glanced over at her, but said nothing.

"I know you're paying for her stay at the boarding house. On a sheriff's wages, that isn't an insignificant thing."

"It's also none of your business. How do you know about that?"

"She let it slip when we were chatting."

"I'm not sure I can trust you again, but I don't know if I'm ready to say goodbye."

"You don't love me."

"What does love have to do with anything?"

"Grace seems to think it means everything."

"What does she know?" He snorted. "She obviously comes from wealth. Hasn't had to think about practical matters."

"She made some excellent points."

Jack and Sarah crept along the mountain ridge and approached the shack as covertly as they could manage. Once they neared the place, they left their horses in relative safety and walked in on foot.

"Grace's horse is gone. They must've taken it." Sarah whispered.

He motioned for her to stay back and he peered in to the building. It was evident a fight had ensued. Grace was lying on the floor still bound to a chair. There was no sign of Calvin or the bandits. He rushed to her side and felt for a pulse. It was faint, but she was alive. Relief surged through him.

He rushed back outside. She's here. They're gone. "Want to give me a hand getting her out of here?"

Sarah followed him in to the shack and looked over Grace. "What did they do to her?"

Jack took in her stained and ripped dress. "I'm not sure I want to know."

Once the two of them cut through the ropes binding Grace. Jack gently lifted her and carried her to his horse.

"You can't make her ride on that beast. Not in her condition."

"What's the difference? She's unconscious."

"I'll ride Bull, you can take Grace on my gelding."

It irritated him that she had a point. Bull was unpredictable on his best days. "Fine."

He gently placed Grace on the grass while he helped Sarah adjust the saddle on Bull. Once Sarah mounted his horse, he settled Grace in front of him on Sarah's Appaloosa. Setting off at a gentle pace, he prayed Doc Murphy was home.

Light filtered through the curtains in the cramped room in Doc Murphy's clinic. Jack had stayed by Grace's bedside throughout the night, but she hadn't returned to them. He wondered if her trauma had been too much to bear. He should have been there. Prevented whatever happened. There had been quite a bit of blood on the shack floor. Had they killed her brother in front of her? He couldn't bear to think what she must've endured. Why had he let her out of his sight?

A faint voice interrupted his thoughts. "Water."

"Grace, thank the Lord you are awake."

"Was I asleep for an extended time?" Her words were barely audible.

"You were unconscious. The doctor called it a coma. It's been about twelve hours since we brought you in."

"May I have some water?"

He poured her a glass from the pitcher Doc had left on the bedside table."

"It's improper for you to be in my room, sheriff."

"Yes. It is." He smiled sheepishly. "But I'm not going anywhere."

"What happened?" she asked.

"I was hoping you could tell me."

"Last thing I remember was a vicious, hulking man walking in. He strode into the hideout demanding to see Calvin. Then he punched him in the face before he turned to me."

"Did you hear where they were taking Calvin?"

"No. I remember they called him Little John and told him I was a gift for him. He ran his gun through my hair. I tried to pull away from it, so he hit me with it."

"Did he do anything else?"

"He tore my dress."

Rage bubbled inside his gut. He'd desired to kill the man who'd dared touch her. Grace looked down at herself and he saw the glint of panic in her eyes as she realized her dress was gone and she wore nightclothes. "What happened to my clothing?"

"Your dress was in tatters. Sarah changed you. I was not in the room."

She let out a relieved sigh. "Tell her thank you for me."

"I will."

Grace admired the profile of Sheriff Garrison as he stared out the window of Dr. Murphy's clinic. She wondered what was causing the grim set of his mouth and the deep creases that appeared in his forehead. She'd been awake for more than an hour and the fact that he lingered in her room all that time came as a surprise. When finally he turned back toward her, she sat upright.

"Was Sarah injured? The last I saw her she was running away to get help."

"Sarah led me to you. She's unharmed."

"What about Buttercup?"

He shook his head. "She wasn't there when we found you."

"Do you think I can go back to the boarding house and visit with Sarah soon?"

"I'll have to ask Doc Murphy. He may want to keep you here under observation."

"I hope not. I'm anxious to leave this place."

"I'll go ask him." He closed the door softly behind him.

Grace could hear muffled voices, but couldn't make out their words. Time dragged on as she waited for Jack to return. Sheriff Garrison. She shouldn't be thinking of him as Jack. It must be Sarah's influence. She was constantly referring to him by his familiar name.

Finally, the door opened and Sheriff Garrison came in with the doctor in tow.

"I'm reluctant to send you back to the boarding house, Miss Belle, but the sheriff claims you are antsy to get back and I admit the friendly faces at there may do you good. I've agreed to allow your release on the condition that Sheriff Garrison stays on the premises for a day or two before leaving you to your own devices. I'll lend the sheriff my wagon to transport you. If there are any changes in your condition, I expect to be notified immediately."

"Thank you, doctor. I'll gladly comply with your wishes, provided that it isn't too much trouble for the sheriff."

"It is, but it's better than hanging around here."

"Who asked you to idle away your time here, anyway?" She asked in a huff.

"You don't have anyone else to look after you."

"I can take care of myself."

"Obviously. That's why I found you unconscious on the floor of that shack."

Grace put her head down so he couldn't see the color she knew was rising into her cheeks.

When Grace entered the room, Sarah jumped up to greet her, ushering her into a chair by the fire. "Grace! You look so much better. I was worried, but Jack insisted I come back here and let the Rutherfords know what happened."

"I will not allow this setback to prevent me from rescuing Calvin."

"Do you think it's wise to go hurrying off again, so soon, after what you've been through?"

"It seems I may have to sneak away while the sheriff sleeps. Dr. Murphy assigned him as my caretaker."

"Jack agreed to keep watch over you?"

"He did. Reluctantly." She sighed. "I am content to release him from the obligation."

"At least wait another night before sneaking away. You should rest after what you've been through."

"Calvin may not have another night."

"We don't know for sure that he's still alive." Sarah spoke the words in a near whisper, but the cut of them wasn't lessened.

"I must keep hope."

Sarah gave her a weak smile. "Pray about it."

"I will pray." Grace let herself relax in the upholstered chair.

Mrs. Rutherford appeared with an unwieldy box.

Sarah jumped up to assist her with it and the two set it down on the floor. "What's this?" she asked.

"The Christmas trimmings." The older woman stood before them. "Grace can sit back and drink some hot cocoa while you and I decorate the boarding house."

"That will be fun. I'll get the cocoa."

Some time later, Sarah came back with cups for the three of them. Mrs. Rutherford had already begun setting up her most prized decoration on the fireplace mantle. It was a crèche featuring the baby Jesus in the manger with Mary and Joseph standing over him. There were farm animals scattered about.

Hours later, Mr. Rutherford appeared with clippings he'd cut from fir trees in the hills. The festive atmosphere was contagious, and ignoring her sore muscles and bruises, Grace assisted in adorning the house. When they completed, the atmosphere was jubilant, reminding Grace of her childhood. She'd spent the last eighteen years despising the trappings of Christmas, but somehow, in this moment, she felt like she was part of a family again. The notion brought a surge of guilt. There was no excuse for making merry with these strangers while her brother remained in danger. She quietly slipped away to her room confident nobody would notice her absence.

Later that night, Grace fingered the Bible on her bedside table. It called her to read and she did. She opened to the book of Isaiah and read about waiting on the Lord. Then she read another verse that reminded her not to fear.

She trudged to the window and stared out at the dark night. God was faithful and had allowed her to be rescued. If it was His will, Calvin would be saved too. It would happen in God's time, not hers. Sometimes, she wished she could prompt Him to work on her timetable, but alas, He knew the end from the beginning and the best thing for her to do was trust in His sovereign grace.

Grace crept down the stairs for a cup of tea. She was not surprised to find Jack in the kitchen. She had no desire to speak with him after his attitude back at the clinic, so she quickly turned away with the intent of heading back to her room.

"Don't go." He spoke the words quietly.

She halted her steps, but didn't turn around. "Why should I stay?"

"I didn't mean what I said at Doc Murphy's place."

She whirled on him and raised her voice. "You meant every word."

"Maybe I did, but I shouldn't have said them."

"I will be going up to my room now."

"You came down for tea. Have some. If one of us needs to go, I will." He waited for her to give some indication of whether he should stay or go and when she didn't, he started for the doorway.

"You may stay if you like." She poured the water from the pitcher into the tea kettle and set it on the hearth.

"The trimmings look nice. The fir tree boughs decorating the staircase have such a pleasant fragrance. Did you assist with the decorating?"

"I did." She turned to face him, keeping the chair between them.

"Where is the mistletoe?" A mischievous grin spread on his face.

"As far as I know, there wasn't any."

"Mrs. Rutherford always hangs mistletoe. She puts it in a different place each year, but you can count on me finding it."

Grace's insides did a strange little flip at the suggestion. She wondered if he was teasing or if he really meant to steal a kiss. The anticipation of such a moment warmed her cheeks, so she turned away to hide her blush.

He walked up behind her and turned her to face him. "We keep battling. Maybe we could attempt to be friends."

"I am not planning to remain in Cimarron."

"Don't be so bristly. You could use another friend. I see you and Sarah have become close, but I can certainly promise you more honesty than she can."

"That is unfair." She turned from him and added tea leaves to the pot, before setting it aside.

"Is it?" He raised a brow.

"It is. Her boss would not allow her to divulge information to you. If she had, she may have been fired."

"Some things come before work."

"Do they? What about for you? Do you put anything ahead of work?" She lifted the tea kettle and poured them each a glass.

"You made your point." He looked appropriately chagrined. "This tea is delicious."

"It looks like hot water, it must not have steeped enough." She smiled.

"I do love this time of year, don't you?"

"No. It is not to my liking."

"Does the cold get to you?"

"I am not that delicate."

"Then why don't you like this time of year?"

"If you must know, we lost our parents a few days before Christmas."

"I am so sorry. I shouldn't have asked."

"You knew not what you were asking." She gave him a sad smile. "Calvin does much to make Christmas special, but it feels like there is a cage around my heart for which I have no key."

"Is not Jesus the key?"

"Yes, but He has not unlocked this particular cage."

"Maybe you haven't given him permission." She could see the wisdom in his words, but instead of comforting her, it annoyed her. It was true that she held this one area of her life back from the Lord. Letting go of the pain was too much to ask, it was all she had left of the mother and father who gave her so much love.

She wondered how a man with such wisdom when it came to her life could be so daft when it came to his own. "Jack, do you really favor convenience over affection and love? Were you honestly planning to marry a woman for whom you had no feelings?"

"Yes, I planned to marry for expedience. I do have feelings for Sarah, they are friendly rather than romantic ones, but they would've grown into more with time, had she not deceived me." He leaned back in his chair and took another tentative sip.

"I know I am being forward, but may I ask why you were not prepared to wait until the feelings grew?"

"I would like children while I am still able to run around after them."

"Does Sarah want children?"

"That was a point of contention."

"You were both settling."

"Yes, I suppose we were."

"Will you still?"

"I cannot be with a woman I do not trust."

"Is that simply an excuse to end a courtship you were unsure about?"

"It might be. If so, I was unaware of it, until now." He put down the delicate tea cup and reached for her hands.

She allowed the intimacy.

"Do you want children, Grace?"

"More than anything."

"Why haven't you wed?"

"I have not been asked."

"You surely had plenty of social opportunities in Philadelphia. Did you attend many parties?"

"A few. I did attend the Vanderbilt Ball back in March, but I have not gone to many parties. I am more of a homebody. I prefer reading to dancing."

"You appear too cultured to have skipped out on social niceties."

"I know not if that is an insult or a compliment coming from you?" She pulled her hands from his.

He walked around the table toward her, then bent down, tucked her hair behind her ear, leaned in close, and whispered, "I'll leave that a mystery."

Jack left the room and she fought the urge to follow him. She wondered what had happened in the last twenty minutes that seemed to change the dynamic of their relationship. He'd gone from treating her as a mere annoyance to treating her as something else entirely. It had to be her imagination. He'd made his feelings about her perfectly clear and she would not allow her silly heart to get in the way. The man didn't even believe in love, at least not the same way she did. Then the object of her thoughts reappeared in the doorway, a grin splitting his handsome face. "I found the mistletoe, so if you don't want me to come upon you under it, you had best beware."

Another flip in her stomach alerted her to how much she hoped that he did find her under the mistletoe.

It was past time she rescued Calvin and made her way home to Philadelphia instead of fantasizing about the strong, virile sheriff.

Chapter Five

*G*race quietly crept down the staircase and paused at the bottom to make sure she hadn't disturbed anyone. After a few seconds, she made her way to the kitchen and quietly opened the back door. The door closed with a bang and she bit her lip to stop herself from muttering in frustration. She waited silently for several minutes to be sure nobody else heard the noise.

Slowly, she crept toward the barn. If she could saddle a horse and make her way back to the shack, maybe she could follow the tracks at first light.

She moved through the dark barn murmuring reassuringly to the horses as she did. She was surprised not to find Bull in the stalls. Maybe Jack had put him out in the pasture for the night or maybe he'd gone home. He certainly didn't have to follow Dr. Murphy's orders to keep a watch over her. Approaching Sarah's Appaloosa, she stroked the horse's neck and placed a blanket on her back. Once she had successfully saddled the horse she put one foot in the stirrup to mount her. A strong arm snaked around her waist and grabbed her from behind. She cried out.

"Where are going, Miss Belle?"

"You startled me, sheriff." She turned to face him, but remained in his arms. His touch sent shivers of delight through her body.

"Is that how it is? I'm back to being sheriff?" He pulled her closer to him. "Earlier you used my familiar name."

"I was matching your level of formality. You addressed me as Miss Belle."

"So I did." He chuckled. "I wish I could say I hadn't expected you to sneak off in the middle of the night, but obviously that would be a lie."

"It would?"

"I'm here waiting for you, aren't I?"

She could barely see his features in the darkness, but she felt the heat smoldering in his touch. Pulling away slightly, so there would be a respectable distance between them, she blinked several times. "Why were you waiting for me? And why not make your presence known when I came into the barn."

"I waited until you saddled a horse, so you couldn't give me some story about what you were doing out here."

"You expected me to lie?"

"Not convincingly. I would've been able to see the truth. I don't believe you have much experience with deception. Do you, Miss Belle?" He leaned down and whispered in her ear. "I can sense the truth in your touch."

She felt her heart race. "What truth is that?"

"You felt something in the kitchen tonight, and now you're running scared. You think if you can find your brother, you will hurry off to Philadelphia and won't have to face your feelings for me."

"I do not know what you are talking about."

He stroked her hair before placing a hand behind her neck and running his thumb along her jawline. "Yes, you do, but fear not." He let out a breath. "As much as I want to take further advantage of our alone time, I won't. It hasn't been a respectable amount of time since I ended my courtship of Sarah, but that doesn't mean I will leave those rosy lips unkissed indefinitely." He ran his thumb along lower lip before releasing her.

She felt something akin to disappointment, but brushed it off. "Thank you." It was the wrong thing to say. Embarrassment warmed her cheeks. She wasn't interested in the handsome sheriff. She had a home and a life to get back to. If she told herself that enough, she might be convinced.

"I won't allow you to take off in the night alone. If you're going, I'm joining you."

"I am going."

"Why don't we take Bull? He's much faster?"

"Speaking of Bull, where is he?"

"He's saddled and waiting for us."

"Don't you think we should be on separate horses?"

"Not if you want to find your brother before Christmas."

"Thank you for doing this. For going with me."

"I am happy to do it, if it keeps you and Sarah from foolishly chasing down leads on your own."

"I do not know how you ever planned to marry a detective if you did not like her doing her job."

"Can we agree that I made a mistake and move on?"

"Yes."

At first light, Jack and Grace carefully inspected the area around the ramshackle building where Grace had so recently been held. Jack watched Grace tense up, then force herself to calm down, so she could accomplish the task at hand. He admired her strength.

"Over here." He pointed to some broken shrubbery. "I think they came through here." He helped Grace to get back onto Bull and then mounted in front of her. "Hang on to me if it gets bumpy."

It was slow going. He was frequently forced to dismount in order to pick out the path the bandits had used. Each time the shrubbery thinned, Jack would spot blood which kept them headed in the direction they'd taken Calvin. He had to wonder how much blood he'd lost. If he was still alive, he wondered if he would remain that way much longer.

"Grace, was your brother able to tell you why he was wanted by these outlaws?"

"Yes."

Bull slid a little down an incline and she clung to his waist. He forced himself to ignore the sensations her touch brought on. "Care to elaborate?"

He could feel her sigh behind him. "He claims he was trying to protect a student who was with child by agreeing to wed her, but the proposed marriage led her father to believe that he was the father of her unborn child. Now her father wants Calvin dead. Having encountered the monster myself, I believe he will kill him, but it wouldn't surprise me if he tortured him first."

"Death seems like an extreme punishment for a premarital dalliance, especially since he was willing to marry the girl."

"My brother is not the type she is permitted to marry."

"Why not?"

"We are not of British descent."

"Seriously?"

She nodded. "Odd, isn't it?"

"Yes. People have their prejudices, but that is a new one to me. What nationality are you, if you don't mind me asking? You do look British? It's what I would've guessed."

"Dutch on our mother's side, French on our father's side."

"Mixed nationalities. No wonder the scoundrel came after Calvin," he joked.

She shoved him, throwing him off balance, but he quickly regained control.

"After seeing the condition Little John left you in, I have to believe he'd do worse to your brother. He'll doubtless kill him if we don't get to him first."

"He was only trying to save the girl from a life of shame."

"If that is true, it was admirable of him."

"I believe him, but even if he were lying, he doesn't deserve to die for it."

"No. He doesn't."

"Over here." He indicated a barely visible trail. "They must've gone this way, see how it's worn down, like someone has been through here more than once?"

She leaned closer to his ear. "Not really, but I'll take your word for it."

As they came around a massive outcropping of rock, Jack hopped down and helped Grace do the same. He peered around a boulder and saw what looked like a homestead.

"Wait here." He briefly grasped her hand before dropping it again. "I'm going to find out if they're here. You can keep look out. Have you ever fired a gun?" She nodded, so he handed her his backup Colt.

"Be careful with it. Don't hesitate to use it if someone tries to grab you." He winked. "Other than me."

Grace lay as still as she could on top of a flat rock that gave her a decent vantage point. She watched Jack approach one window and then another before finally opening a door and entering the dwelling. It wasn't much, but it seemed to be well cared for with a few plants around the adobe house.

When Jack reappeared it was from around the far side of the building. He slowly and cautiously made his way toward her. "There was a struggle in there. We'll need to figure out what direction they traveled when they left here."

She sat up and buried her face in her hands. "Calvin has to be all right. I need him to come home. I can't go back home by myself and I have nobody else."

She felt the warmth of his hand as he placed it on her back. "What about the rest of your family?"

She looked up into his eyes. "My parents died days apart when I was ten. Tuberculosis. My brother is the only close family I have."

"No aunts and uncles? Cousins?"

"Some. We aren't close."

"I'm sorry." He pulled her into his chest and she let herself be comforted. "We'll find him. You won't have to go home alone."

She knew he had no way of knowing if his words were true, but he made it sound like a promise. Somehow, in that moment, he managed to make her feel protected.

After several minutes past, she lifted her head and dragged herself from his arms. "I'm sorry I fell apart."

"You shouldn't apologize for being human."

She'd do well to remember that even though her silly heart allowed her to read more into his kindness, he was simply comforting a woman in need. Jack was doing his job. He did not care for her personally. Now if she could convince herself not to become infatuated with the kind sheriff she might return home with her heart unscathed.

Jack noticed Grace's sudden change in demeanor. He should be concentrating on finding the trail, but instead he was trying to figure out what he'd said to irritate her. It seemed the two of them couldn't have a simple conversation without one of them offending the other. If he was being honest, it was usually him doing the rankling. He wondered what it was about her that had him uttering ill-advised remarks so often. He genuinely liked her and wanted to be friends, but he kept pushing her away.

He considered Sarah. The two of them had an easy camaraderie. So what if she was more of a pal than a woman he desired romantically? He'd believed it would be enough. At least he had until

Grace came along. What had he been thinking? And would Sarah forgive him for backing away from their courtship? He recalled the words she'd spoken yesterday as they rode out to save Grace. She may have already accepted that it was over. He wondered what had given her the idea that he was interested in Grace. He'd not shown any blatant interest. He might have a passing notion run through his head or a jolt of desire every time her hand touched his, but he certainly had no intention of acting on those feelings. Besides, she planned to return to Philadelphia and he had no interest in going there, so the two of them couldn't have a future. Even if he wanted one. Which he didn't. Did he?

He forced his attention back on the trail and finally found some disturbances he could follow, but every time Grace brushed against him, he was back in his head wondering what to do about his growing attraction to her. He breathed in the light scent of honeysuckle that permeated the air whenever she was close. He should have listened when she'd suggested they take separate horses. He could've had her use Sarah's horse. The only reason he'd had her ride with him on Bull was to keep her close. He could try to fool himself, but it was plain as day.

Then as they approached the mountain ridge, he saw it. Smoke. "There's a fire up ahead. We're going to need to approach on foot. Too risky to ride in on Bull."

"Let's go."

"Maybe you should stay here."

"Why? I want to help."

"You may prove to be more of a hindrance than a help if you keep distracting me." There he went again opening his big mouth and annoying her.

Her spine stiffened. "I think I can manage to avoid distracting you. It is my brother they are holding."

"Let's go." He handed her the revolver again and moved quietly along the ridge toward the smoke.

She tapped his shoulder. When he met her gaze she pointed. He looked to where she indicated and saw that a man was tied to a tree.

"We may be able to get him without disturbing anyone," she said.

"I doubt that. I'm sure someone is on guard. Let's check it out." They quietly looped around to get close enough to survey the situation. Sure enough there were two guards. One had drifted off, but the other was alert and playing with a deck of cards. "I'm going to knock him out as quietly as I can, but if it's not done correctly it can either kill him or make an awful lot of noise alerting anyone who happens to be close."

"Is it necessary?"

"Unfortunately, it's the safest course of action."

"I'll be directly behind you," she said.

It took only a few seconds for him to disable the first guard and relieve him of his weapon. He moved to the sleeping guard and did the same.

Taking his knife out of his pocket, he cut the ropes binding the other man to the tree. He told Calvin to stay silent before removing the gag.

"Let's get out of here before they realize you're gone," he whispered.

The three of them made it back to Bull within ten minutes, but as they approached the stallion he realized carrying three people was asking quite a bit of his horse. "We're not far from the Hayes' Ranch. I'm sure they'll have horses we can borrow, Bull can get us that far.

"I hadn't considered how we would get back if we rescued Calvin."

"Obviously, neither did I, proving once again that I can't think straight around you."

He saw her smile spread at the mention of his mushy brain. She was cute when she gloated.

They gathered in the living room of the boarding house. Jack stood at the window staring into the darkness. He may have brought trouble on the Rutherfords and the other boarding house guests by bringing Calvin here. The options were limited. If he took him to the St. James or even back to his place, that would mean leaving Grace behind.

Calvin broke the silence. "Is my presence putting everyone here in danger?"

Jack turned from the window. "The danger would be present regardless of where we took you." He grimaced. "They will easily discern where Grace is staying and use her to get to you. Sarah's involvement makes her a target, as well.

"So, you're saying there is no way to protect my sister and Miss Jones from my presence?"

"That's not what I'm suggesting. I'm saying we have a better chance of keeping everyone safe if we stay together than we do if we separate."

"Do you plan to stay here and wait for them to attack?"

"Not exactly. I'm going to send a telegram and help will be on the way. With any luck, my friends will arrive before the bandits do."

"How far away are they?"

"Two and a half days, but if I need urgent assistance, they'll make it in half that time."

Mr. Rutherford stood. "I'll go into town to the telegraph office. Wouldn't want you leaving the womenfolk without protection. An aged man like me won't be much benefit in a fight anyway."

"We can manage it, George. You don't have to go."

"Yes, I do. You stay here and protect Eleanor."

"Of course." Jack gave Mr. Rutherford the information he needed for sending the telegram. Then he sat on the sofa beside Grace. He laced his fingers with hers and ran circles on her palm with his thumb. Her little intake of breath gave him some assurance that she felt something more than friendship for him. If he let himself forget that she was leaving, he would fall for her.

"Thank you, Jack. For saving my brother."

"I didn't do it alone."

"I could not have found that place without your tracking skills."

"There are other trackers in the area. Some even better than me."

"And with what should I pay?"

"Why would you pay?" He dropped her hand. Did she think he wanted some kind of payment from her? "I'm the sheriff. I was doing my job." It wasn't exactly his job to find missing adults, but he wasn't about to let her know that she was in any way special after her comment about money.

Calvin paced. "Maybe we should come up with a defense in case they show up before our backup arrives."

"Why don't you and I go to your room to plan and leave the womenfolk down here to relax without having to fret the details?"

"Sure. Let's do that."

Calvin accompanied Jack as he made his way up the wide staircase.

Grace placed her hands on her hips. "What did I do to offend you?"

"I don't know what you're talking about." Jack sat across from her as she filled his teacup.

"That is an outright lie. You dropped my hand earlier as if it had scorched you."

He sneered. "I don't need payment, Miss Belle, not your cash or your affections. As I said, I was doing my job."

"You think I would share my affections in that way? Do you think me a harlot?"

He looked her in the eye. "What was that talk about payment?"

"It was about hiring a tracker. Perfectly clear in the context unless you were looking to misconstrue my words. It had nothing to do with you and me. I didn't expect to make any kind of payment to you, and if I did it certainly would not be through my favors." The idea of marrying him had crossed her mind, and even gained in appeal, until he started acting like a mule.

He leaned back in his chair. "Will you be leaving then? Going back to Philadelphia?"

She turned her back to him and sidled up to the sink. "I'm sure Calvin plans to send for funds, so we can get return tickets to Philadelphia."

"You're planning to leave?" he whispered.

A strong desire washed over her. She wished he'd ask her to stay, but the idea was ridiculous. He'd not given her any indication that he might consider a life with her. "That was always my plan." Why should she remain in town? A few light touches and hand holding did not a romance make.

"I can purchase your return tickets."

Her stomach sank. He was in more of a hurry to get rid of her than she'd realized.

Chapter Six

ack saw Nate and Harry coming from his position on the front porch of the boarding house. He sauntered down the steps to greet them.

"Thanks for coming."

They walked to the stables and Jack fetched the horses water before Harry let them out to graze in the pasture. He stood at the fence watching them.

"Where's the stable boy?" Nate asked.

"Peter's been unwell, but he seems to be recovering slowly."

"Sorry to hear he's been sick, but glad he's getting better. He's a nice young man."

"So, why don't you tell me what's got you paranoid that someone is going to ransack the boarding house?"

"I'm worried they'll attack here if they know that's where Grace and Sarah have been staying."

"They're staying here? Together?"

"It seems they've become close friends."

"Interesting. That didn't take long at all." Nate scratched the side of his head. "Have you picked one yet?"

"It isn't a matter of picking one. I'm not courting Grace." He lifted his eyes from the ground to meet Nate's gaze. "She's in a hurry to get back to Philadelphia."

"Convince her to stay."

"I don't think I could, even if I wanted to."

"Do you want her to stay?"

"I wish I knew my own mind where she was concerned."

"I've got to meet this girl who has you flummoxed."

"Let's go then." Jack tromped up the stairs and into the house with Nate and Harry following behind. He wasn't surprised when Grace and Sarah were both in the living room whispering to each other. "Nate and Harry. I'm sure you both remember Miss Sarah Jones from when she saved our hides in the Glenn Ricketts raid."

Harry walked over to her with an outstretched hand. "Glad to see you again, Miss Jones." He took her hand in his and placed a kiss on the back of it.

"Her friend here is Miss Grace Belle." Harry repeated the procedure, kissing her hand.

Nate tipped his hat. "Good to see you, Miss Jones. Nice to meet you, Miss Belle."

Calvin came down the stairs looking like a new man.

"Calvin here is the reason we're in this mess." Jack glanced up at him with an amiable grin.

"I am. Sorry about the trouble I've caused." Calvin smiled sheepishly.

"We live for trouble. It gives us purpose," Nate said.

"Aren't you about to be a father?" Jack asked.

"I am. Reason enough to survive this."

"Harry, make sure Nate is out of the way when the bullets start flying."

Grace's hand flew to her chest. "Surely you are not expecting a gun fight."

"We're hoping to avoid one, and if we can't, we'd like to keep it some distance from the house."

Grace entered the alcove in the dining room to get the silver and china from the buffet. She sensed Jack approaching and remained still as he walked up behind her and brushed a stray hair from her neck. He stroked her neck with his thumb, sending little jolts of desire through her. She turned to face him and his eyes looked up at the mistletoe hanging above them. Her body tensed in preparation for his kiss and she licked her bottom lip. Her ability to resist him had long since fled. There was no way that she would stop him if he followed through on his threat. His raw, masculine scent was intoxicating.

"What's going on in here?" Sarah giggled when she saw the mistletoe. "Go for it, sheriff."

Grace wiggled out of the space between Jack and the buffet table and ran to the kitchen. She'd come close to having a private moment with Jack in front of the woman he'd nearly married. It was time to go home before her infatuation grew into something more and she ended up with a broken heart.

Sarah joined her in the kitchen. "It's not going to hurt me if you and Jack get together."

"He was teasing me. I do not think he has any interest. Not really."

"Jack isn't the type to play with a woman's emotions."

"I am not so sure."

"I've seen how he looks at you, Grace. Especially when he thinks nobody is watching. I told you how jealous I was Thanksgiving night. He's never looked at me that way. I messed up, but you could make him happy. I care for him and hope he finds love. Even if it's with you instead of me. Besides, your brother has made his intention to pursue me abundantly clear."

"Calvin and you?"

"Is that a problem?"

"No. I think it is fabulous.""So, will you consider what I said about Jack's feelings for you?"

"You are imagining things. I am nothing more to him than a distraction. He has called me as much."

"Maybe you're assumptions are correct, but how will you know for sure if you don't tell him how you feel?"

"I am not even sure how I feel."

"Yet, it's so obvious to everyone else."

Jack was positioned near the road, leaning against a wooden fence post. Night had long since fallen and it was tranquil. His thoughts turned again to Grace. The woman was distracting. She had curves in all the right places and full lips he longed to kiss. It made no sense for him to obsess over her. He couldn't measure up to the wealthy men she must be used to. Her style and finery were that of an affluent lady, not the kind of woman who would settle down in the territories. If he had a dash of wisdom, he would keep his hands and his lips off of her, yet, doing so was inconceivable.

When she looked at him with a longing that matched his own yearning, fighting off his desire was pure torture. The woman had no idea the effect she had on him, and he imagined if she did, she might enjoy the power she held over him.

The sound of a branch breaking alerted him to trouble, pulling him from his reverie. Scanning the area for an intruder, he spotted a heifer that had escaped the fence. It took a moment before he realized that the escaped cow was cause for alarm. Someone must've cut the fence, as he and Nate had inspected the length of it earlier in the day.

He made his way to the stable where Nate was positioned and alerted him to the possible disturbance.

The sound of the creaky back door put him on edge. They made their way toward the house and he spotted Grace outlined against the open door, he lunged for her, pushing her back inside, but not releasing her. "Stay inside," he growled.

She whispered, "Why? Is something wrong?"

His muscles were tense and knew he was frightening her, but she should be afraid. Not only of the outlaws he suspected were outside, but of him. She didn't pull away from his unyielding embrace. "We have trouble out there. I need you to stay inside and move away from the door. Will you do that for me?" He spoke the words quietly, still holding her tightly.

When he felt her nod against his chin, he finally, reluctantly released her and hurried back outside to confront the danger.

He caught up with Nate along the fence line and the other man pointed to the cut fence. "It was definitely tampered with. They have to be here somewhere. Let's go find them."

A sound from the other side of the field got their attention and Nate ran quickly toward it. A gunshot rang out and Jack prayed that Harry and Nate were both safe as he sped toward the sound, he only made it a few steps when a mammoth of a man emerged from the house with an arm around Grace's waist and a gun to her head. He was expected to protect her, but once again he'd failed.

Grace fought against the enormous, bloodthirsty man, but his strength was formidable. Her nostrils were filled with his foul odor. She spotted Jack approaching and prayed he would turn and run for his life, but she knew better. He would fight to the death to protect his friends. Her antics had put him in danger. If she'd only stayed in her room, Little John would not have captured her so easily.

If there was ever a time to trust God, this was it. Fervent prayers passed her lips, so that the behemoth holding her was forced to cover her mouth to stop them. She bit his hand while continuing to send silent prayers upward. The man stumbled backward and fell to the floor. She turned around and saw Nate standing there with a knife dripping with blood. Her eyes turned again to Little John, his throat had been slit. She covered her face with her hands.

Strong arms turned her around and she was crushed to the sheriff's chest. "Shh. You're safe," Jack murmured. Her tears soaked his shirt, but he didn't seem to mind. He held her close for several moments before releasing her. He lifted her chin and met her gaze. "It's going to be all right."

"Hold me." She whispered the plea.

He obliged, pulling her back into his strong arms. After some time passed, Nate reminded them of his presence. "I hate to interrupt, but we need to check on Harry. That gunshot came from his position."

Grace pulled away from Jack and gathered her wits. "Please see if Harry is out of harm's way. I'll clean up this blood."

"Don't touch the crime scene, Grace. I need to document it before we call Doc to come take the body away. Go get Calvin and Sarah and wait with them. Have your brother inspect the inside. I gave him a revolver. He'll be able to protect you if any more trouble arises in there." She hoped no other miscreants were creeping about the house.

Jack approached Harry's last known position. He discovered a dead man with a gun in his hand and bullet in his chest. The body was Harry's size and build, holding his breath, he leaned in close to inspect his face. Relief washed over him. It was one of the guards he'd knocked out during Calvin's rescue. He heard a scuffle near the barn, so he silently crept around the property to assess any remaining danger.

Harry struggled to control an outlaw. Nate entered the stable and helped Harry to tie the man up.

Jack saw the glint of light on the rifle barrel before he noticed the man holding it, but before the bandit could pull the trigger, he was on the ground. At the sound of the gunshot, Harry and Nate both looked up at him. Their relief at his timing was apparent.

Four outlaws had come for the Belles, but only one would have the privilege of a trial. Jack approached the other men and immediately recognized their prisoner as Elmer Severil. "You still eligible to collect bounties, Nate?"

"Sure am."

"There's a decent one on our friend, Elmer, here. He was involved in that stage coach robbery near you. Sarah was working a case for the Pinkertons trying to recover the loot." It hit him then that Edward was involved in that same heist. Sarah had shared what she was able, but left out the most important detail.

He considered Little John's daughter, and sympathized for her loss. The pain of losing his brother was fresh and cut deep. He hoped she would be able to give her child a sheltered life, away from the malefactors her father was known to consort with.

Jack took the package from the mail bag that came on the stage coach and stuffed it in the pocket of his jacket. A sharp pain in his chest reminded him that he didn't want Grace to leave town. He could ask her to stay, but that wouldn't be fair to her. She didn't have any desire to live in the wilds of the territory. Her place was in Philadelphia. Her home there had running water. No. It wasn't fair to ask her to stay in this primitive town.

He slowed Bull's usual pace on the trip to the boarding house. It felt like the end and he wanted to prolong it. Maybe she would ask him to join her. He had no idea what he would do with himself in a big city, but he would make it work if she wanted him by her side. It was no use fantasizing about her. The time had come to give Calvin the tickets and have the two of them leave town before his heart betrayed him further.

Bringing Bull to halt, he stared at the vision on the porch of the boarding house. She was beautiful. Her golden hair was tightly wound in a perfect updo. He longed to release the pins holding it and feel the silky strands between his fingers.

"Sheriff." She gave a little nod of greeting.

"Hello, Miss Belle."

A tentative smile played at the edge of her lips. "Glad you came by."

"Are you now?" He couldn't stop his grin.

"Will you be staying for dinner or do you have to rush off again?"

"I might be persuaded to stay."

"Wonderful." She sashayed into the house and out of sight.

He sucked in a breath and led Bull to the stables. Stroking his long neck, he murmured to his faithful steed. "She's about the prettiest thing I ever saw, but we have to let her go. I know you'll miss her, but we need to think about her needs first." He looked into the horses eyes as if expecting an answer, before removing his saddle and letting him out into the pasture to graze.

As he exited the stable, Peter shuffled past him with a bucket of water in each hand. "Howdy, sheriff."

"Glad to see you up and around."

"Thanks." Peter beamed from ear to ear. "They say I've been out of it for a long while. I don't remember much."

"That might be a blessing. The Rutherford's feared they'd lose you for a few days there. It was a scary time."

"I'm glad to be up and about again."

"God is great."

"Indeed." Peter set a water bucket in each of the occupied stalls. "Would you like me to round up Bull and brush him down for you?"

"He'll be fine. I think he's more hungry than anything else."

"I can get him some oats."

"That would be fantastic. Thanks."

When Jack finally made his way into the house, the clatter of silver greeted him as the three women bustled about setting the table. Mrs. Rutherford gave him a wink and patted his shoulder as she hustled past him. He wondered what she was hinting at.

He walked through the kitchen and out the back door, hoping to clear his head before the meal was served. He tried not to listen to the conversation in the kitchen, but it was impossible to block out the voices, and when he heard his name, his curiosity got the better of him and he listened intently.

"Grace, tell Jack how you feel." Sarah said.

"You know I cannot do that. It would be most inappropriate." Came Grace's sweet voice. Did this mean she cared for him too? Was he acting a fool by sending her away?

Grace stepped through the back door hoping to escape Sarah for a moment. Her eyes widened when she noticed Sheriff Garrison standing beside the door. "How much did you hear?"

He took a step closer and ran the tip of his index finger from the nape of her neck down her neck and along her collar bone. She tried to force herself to breathe normally, but his touch rendered it impossible.

"Jack?"

He placed his hand in the crook of her arm and walked her away from the house. When they were a safe distance away and hidden behind an outbuilding, he stopped and faced her. "Is what Sarah said true?"

"So you *were* listening?"

"I heard."

She wondered if he felt the same or if he wanted her to leave. Why wouldn't he say something? She stared at him waiting for some response.

"You are beautiful."

"But?"

"Why must there be a 'but'?

"There is always a but."

"But you don't belong here."

"Oh." She turned away and started back toward the house, but he grabbed her arm and spun her around before she made it two steps.

He bit his lip as he stared down at her. She anticipated the kiss she knew was coming. As he bent his head closer to hers, she braced herself for the onslaught of sensations, but before his lips met hers, the dinner bell rang.

Jack groaned. "We will continue this." The twinkle in his eyes let her know he meant what he said.

Dinner seemed to go on forever. She wanted to escape the room and spend time with Jack, but her impeccable manners would not allow such impulsive behavior. When the meal was cleaned up after and the dinner guests had dispersed to their rooms, she looked around, but Jack was nowhere to be found. It was probably for the best. His actions had been inviting, but his words had been harsh. He made it clear that he expected her to go home where she belonged. It was foolish for her to want to share kisses with a man who had no intention of keeping her around. She retired to her room and allowed herself the luxury of daydreaming about Jack Garrison and what it would be like to be held in his arms and to have his lips capture hers. She had yet to experience a romantic kiss, but could easily imagine the feelings. They had to be similar to what she was experiencing presently.

After some time, she roamed to her window and stared out into the night. To her surprise, she saw Calvin and Jack outside talking together. Then she saw Jack hand her brother a package.

Her curiosity got the better of her and she joined them outside to see what they were discussing and what was in the package.

Calvin turned to greet her as the door swung open. "Little sister, I have fantastic news."

"Oh?"

"Sheriff Garrison has provided tickets for our return trip to Philadelphia. We can be home in time for Christmas."

"Did he now?" A sinking feeling filled her. It was true. He wanted her to go. She gave Jack a withering look before turning on her heel and storming back into the house.

Chapter Seven

"Grace, wait."

"I think I would rather be alone, sheriff."

"I bought the tickets more than a week ago."

"You gave them to Calvin tonight. After you knew how I felt."

"I'm still not sure how you feel." He reached for her hand, but she pulled away.

"Please. Grace. Can we talk?"

"I want to be alone. Please leave."

He turned away and back out the front door past Calvin and headed to the stable.

As he saddled Bull, he considered what Grace said. It was true. He had passed those tickets along to Calvin understanding full well that Grace would stay if he proposed. His motives were pure. Was it not noble to want to send her back to the comforts of home, back to the world she knew and loved? Asking her to stay would be beyond selfish. He mounted the stallion and headed for home. Night had descended and the penetrating chill made riding difficult.

If he was smart, he would avoid Grace Belle and her brother until they were gone. At the last moment, when his house came into view, he turned the horse the other way and headed for the office. There was no way sleep would come, so he might as well get some work done. Maybe there was a lawbreaker or two hanging around the saloon waiting to be arrested.

Two hours later, the front door of the saloon opened and Calvin Belle rushed through the doors. The man hurried over to his table.

"Is there something I can help you with Calvin?"

"Yes, sheriff."

"How did you know where to find me?"

"I didn't. You weren't at your house and you weren't at your office, so I figured I should try here."

"Here I am. What can I do for you?"

"It's about Sarah."

"What about her? Is she hurt?"

"No. Nothing like that."

"She and I have been spending some time together. Tonight, I learned about you courting her and realized I was out of line. I apologize."

"Sarah and I are no longer anything more than friends. It was mutual." An eyebrow shot up. "I'm surprised she didn't tell you that."

"She wasn't the one who told me about your relationship."

"Grace?"

Calvin nodded.

"I hurt her."

He nodded again. "Yes. You did."

"So, it's okay if I ask Sarah to marry me?"

"Wow. You work fast."

"She's an amazing woman. I would love to spend my life with a woman like her."

"Then I guess congratulations are in order."

"Not unless she agrees."

"Good luck, Calvin."

"I don't believe in luck, so I'd rather have your prayers."

"You've got it." Jack watched as Calvin exited the saloon. Calvin's words weighed heavily on him. Why hadn't he considered praying about his feelings for Grace? What had happened to his faith in past few weeks to make him stray so far that God wasn't foremost on his mind and in his heart?

When he got home that night, he fell to his knees beside his bed and poured his heart out to the Lord. When he finally crawled into bed, sleep quickly overtook him.

Grace boarded the train without a backwards glance. She would force herself to return to Philadelphia. Finding her seat, she stowed her carpet bag and sat down. Calvin scooted in beside her. The train cars were uncomfortable, but at least on the journey home, she would have her brother's protection.

When they got home, she would throw herself into the social scene. She normally chose to skip most of the parties and balls in Philadelphia, but would try to assimilate this time. It was time for her to embrace the trappings of life in the city. She needed to find a hobby since a husband and children were not going to materialize out of nowhere. Calvin had assured her their parents' wealth was intact and she would never be required to find employment. He explained that when she married or left home she would receive a sizable portion of the estate, which meant there was no excuse for her to wallow in self-pity. God had blessed her beyond measure, financially and otherwise. It was time for her to accept His answer when it came to Jack.

She should be celebrating Calvin's rescue and his upcoming nuptials. A smile played at the corners of her mouth. Who would have guessed that Calvin and Sarah would hit it off so quickly? She stared out the window of the train. If only Jack could attend the wedding with her. She wished there was a way to erase him from her memories. Then again, she wanted to remember everything about him: his scent, his touch, his voice, no matter how painful it was.

When the train began to move, she would've sworn she'd seen Jack riding up on Bull. Maybe it was him. Or maybe she was imagining him. He could've been there for something else, or someone else. He certainly wouldn't have ridden two days journey to catch up with her. He'd made his position clear. There was no place for her in Cimarron.

"Calvin?"

"Yes?"

"When will Sarah be joining us?"

"If the train is on time, she'll arrive the Saturday before Christmas."

"Will you marry immediately?"

"As soon as the wedding of her dreams can be planned."

Grace turned toward the window. "Do you think the staff decorated for Christmas?"

"Most definitely." He placed a hand on her shoulder. "Since when do you trouble yourself with Christmas?"

"I am not troubled about it."

"I think you might be."

Jack watched the train pull away as a lump formed in his throat. He'd missed her. Having bought her ticket himself, he knew what time the train would leave, yet he'd missed it.

Bull snorted. "We'll go to Pa's and you can have a break, maybe you'll even get to visit that mare you've had your eye on." He would ride another horse back to town, so Bull could rest.

After dropping off Bull at his father's place, he rented a horse from the livery. He headed back to the train station and approached the counter.

"When is the next train to Philadelphia?"

"There are no direct trains from here to there." The man behind the counter replied.

"I'm aware of that. Is it possible for me to make it to Philadelphia before Christmas?"

"I can get you there on December 22nd."

"Perfect." He would be cutting it close if anything delayed the train, but if the journey proceeded smoothly, he could be with Grace for Christmas. If she'd have him. The thought that she might send him away had his stomach tied up in knots. What had he been thinking letting her leave without telling her how he felt? He felt foolish.

His friend's voice interrupted his thoughts. "What brings you to Santa Fe?"

"Howdy, Nate."

"That didn't answer my question."

"Chasing after a woman."

"That Grace Belle has a hold on you, doesn't she?"

"She's gone."

"Then follow her."

He held out the tickets for Nate to inspect.

"Harry's supposed to take a few days off, but I'm sure he won't mind if I spend Christmas in Cimarron, so the rival gangs see that law and order doesn't take a holiday."

"I'm not sure I'm coming back, Nate. If she'll have me, I will stay."

"What about Cimarron?"

"I've been thinking about asking Peter to deputy for me. I haven't done so yet, but maybe you could."

"The Rutherford's stable boy?"

"He's of slight build, but he's eighteen. He deserves the chance to prove himself. He's always wanted to be a lawkeeper. Maybe Harry can take him on as a deputy and you can take over in Cimarron."

"I can interim for you, but there will need to be a special election. That town cannot function without the law."

"I know. It's a tough decision. I'm torn between doing what is best for Cimarron and marrying Grace."

"Why can't you do both? Bring her back here."

"She couldn't be happy here."

"She seemed happy to me."

"That was when she knew she was going home."

"Maybe you should ask her. Let her make her own decisions. I'll support you in whatever you decide." Nate slapped him on the back. "I got some new information you might find interesting."

"What would that be?"

"It's about Little John's daughter, Maria. She married the father of her unborn child."

"Interesting. I heard the father ran off."

"He did, but he's back. When her father found out about the baby, Maria hid the relationship and gave Calvin's name to protect her lover. Her lies snowballed out of control."

"How did you learn all this?"

"The circuit preacher who performed my marriage to Adeline performed theirs. He came to the sheriff's office looking for a witness. Naturally, I had questions for the young woman before agreeing."

"That girl will live with the guilt of her father dying as a result of that lie."

"Yes, I'm sure she will, but that circuit preacher is a great witness for the Lord, and if she allows Him too, Jesus would surely release her from her burden of guilt. Besides, didn't Little John die as a result of his own poor decisions? Such as grabbing Grace?" Nate asked.

"Definitely."

"Imagine how she would've felt if she'd known the man she asked to witness her wedding was the sheriff who slit her father's throat."

"I take it you left out that little detail?" Jack asked.

"She only knows her father died in an attempted attack on Calvin. It wouldn't benefit her to know the details."

"I would think not."

"You'd better go pack. You have a rough journey ahead."

"How bad can train travel be?"

"Brutal." Nate grinned. "Stuffed in a cramped compartment with smelly passengers and overheated cabins. Let's not forget the bouncing train car knocking your vertebrae out of place."

"Something to look forward to. Thanks for that"

"Anytime."

"How's Addy?"

"She's still bustling about. After Christmas, she'll stay at Pa's ranch until the baby comes in February, that way she'll have help if she needs it and won't be alone if she goes into labor. Rosa has midwifing skills, so I trust that Adeline is safe in her capable hands."

"Perfect. I feel better about asking you to take over for me in Cimarron, it's much closer to your father's ranch than Santa Fe."

"That it is."

"Can you do me one more favor?"

"What would that be?"

"Get Bull to your father's ranch. I left him at my Pa's since he needs a break. We rode hard to get here."

"I'll ride him there. I wouldn't trust him not to hurt anyone else."

"That's why I'm asking you."

"If you stay in Philadelphia, you'll be missed."

"Don't get emotional."

Nate laughed. "I won't. I'm off to get Harry caught up. Tell Grace I hope to see her again someday." Nate ambled off, while Jack stared down the railroad tracks, what-if questions flooding his mind.

Grace sat quietly in the pew beside Calvin as the preacher spoke of a coming revival. Her heart ached, but she knew God would provide for her needs. He may not allow her to have her heart's desire, but His love would be enough. All she had to do was put Him first. Everything else would fall into place the way He planned. Giving up control was a daily struggle. One day she would promise the Lord that she would trust His plan, and the following day would find her worrying needlessly over matters out of her control.

After the message, she slowly made her way outside. It would take time and faith for her broken heart to mend.

Calvin assisted her as she climbed into the carriage. He climbed in beside her, put his arm around her and squeezed. "You won't feel this way forever, Grace. It wasn't meant to be. The right man will come along."

"Forgive me if I have my doubts."

"Jack is a decent man, and I can see how his kindness could've been misconstrued for more, but his life is in the territories and you would never have been happy there."

"He would have made me happy."

"Joy must come from God."

"Do you think me a simpleton? I know from where my joy should arise." She turned and watched the road filled with other carriages and foot traffic. "I cannot help how I feel. He kept my heart with him in Cimarron."

"I wish there was something I could do to ease your pain."

"There is." She looked him in the eye. "Find me something to do. I cannot remain idle."

"You could take over the philanthropic endeavors. The next event is a charity ball. It is set for Saturday, but there remain details to be managed."

"I will attend to it."

"Perfect. I think that type of work will suit you."

"Calvin?"

"Yes?"

"Thank you." She gave him a weak smile. "I know you want what is best for me."

"In time it will get better. You'll see."

Jack boarded the train and took his seat. The overheated cabin was cramped and left little room for stretching his long legs. He held his worn Bible on his lap. After realizing how far he'd strayed from God, he'd purposed in his heart to spend time in the Word each day. If he continually sought God, he was convinced that the Lord would provide him with the direction he needed.

He was startled when Sarah took the seat beside him. "I'm surprised to see you, Sarah. Where are you headed?"

Color rose to her cheeks. "Calvin Belle asked me to be his wife."

"He mentioned he'd planned to do so."

"I'm going to Philadelphia." She smiled knowingly. "I assume you're doing the same."

"You assume correctly."

"Why did you let her leave?"

"Guilt." He sighed. "I couldn't bring myself to take her away from everything she knew and loved."

"She would've given it up for you. She told me as much."

"You two really did form a bond quickly."

"Now she will be my sister."

"If she agrees to marry me does that make *you* my sister?"

Her musical laugh filled the air. "I reckon that it does, sheriff."

"I apologize for my reaction on Thanksgiving."

She placed a hand on his cheek. "No. I'm sorry. I should have told you about Edward."

"Yes, you should've, but it was no excuse for my behavior."

"Will you forgive me, Jack?"

"Yes. Will you do me the same courtesy?"

"Done. You will always have a place in my heart, Jack."

"Don't make this ride any more awkward than it already is."

She laughed again. "Grace is a lucky woman."

"And Calvin is a lucky man."

"Neither one of them would call it luck, you know."

"No?"

"They would both say they were blessed."

"That may be accurate. Calvin is indirectly responsible for my spending more quality time with God."

"How so?"

"After asking my permission to court you," he winked, "I wished him luck, but he asked me to pray for him. It wasn't so much his words, but the way he said them. It got me to thinking and I realized I hadn't prayed about the situation with you or with Grace."

The silence stretched between them, but it wasn't awkward. He reflected on the months they'd spent together. She was an amazing woman, and he hoped she found true happiness in Philadelphia. The Pinkerton Agency had an office there, so he was sure she could continue in her vocation. It was important, worthwhile work that she did.

At the station in Philadelphia, Jack disembarked and helped Sarah with her bags. "Do you know where we're going?"

"A carriage will pick us up. Then we must dress quickly, we have a charity ball to attend."

"I don't have to attend. They don't even know I'll be here."

"Don't you want to make Grace's night? She'll be there alone if you don't show up."

"Maybe another man escorted her there."

"No. Grace wouldn't allow anyone else to accompany her, except possibly Calvin."

"No pressure?"

Sarah grinned. "I'm sure Calvin has something that will fit you, the two of you are around the same size."

"How do you know I don't have clothes for the occasion?"

"Your bag is too small to fit much, Jack." She reached for his arm. "Here's our ride."

The two of them loaded into the carriage. Within minutes, they'd arrived at an enormous Victorian home. A man, he presumed was a butler took their bags at the door, but didn't ask any questions. "Sir, if you'll follow me, I'll show you to your room." He was taken to one wing of the house and he watched as Sarah was led to a room in the other direction. After settling his belongings in his room, he descended the grand staircase and began the search for Calvin.

"Jack! I can't believe you're here." Calvin's voice boomed from behind him.

He turned to face the other man. "May we speak a moment?"

"Definitely, come into the library. I'll have coffee brought in."

"That sounds heavenly."

Once they'd settled in with coffee and pastries, Jack began, "I've come to ask for your sister's hand in marriage. May I have your blessing?"

Calvin whistled, letting the sound out slowly. "You have no idea how happy that makes me."

"Why is that?"

"She's been pining over you since we left. I didn't think you felt the same, so I've been trying to convince her to forget about you. I even set her in charge of running the philanthropic endeavors our parents started, but her heart isn't in it. She's setting up for the charity ball now, but later you'll find her holding up the walls."

"Does she not dance?"

"She's a fine dancer, but if I were to guess, she's standing around waiting for Sarah and I to show up and praying we're on time."

"I didn't bring finery for attending a ball."

"Fret not, I'll have clothes brought in for you. The staff can make any necessary adjustments."

"On another subject, I have a bit of news for you," Jack said.

"What would that be?"

"Maria married the child's father."

"That is wonderful news. I'd been agonizing over my decision to marry Sarah when I'd promised myself to Maria."

"You're free, Calvin." Jack smiled. He would spare the other man the details of how Maria had caused the whole fiasco with her lies.

He glanced around the room admiring the floor to ceiling bookshelves loaded with books that adorned three of the walls. He was sure it must be Grace's favorite room.

"I assumed Grace came from a wealthy family, but I didn't expect anything like this place."

Calvin laughed. "Nobody does. Our mother was a Vanderbilt. It's not something we advertise."

"That's wise." Jack smiled wryly.

"It worked. The two of us will both marry for love, not because someone was attracted to our money."

Jack looked down at his feet before looking the other man in the eye. "I regret I didn't tell Grace how I felt before she left."

"I'm sure you will make it up to her."

"For the rest of our lives."

Chapter Eight

race stood near the grand windows in the elaborate ballroom. She'd convinced herself to attend this charity ball. Now she stood by cinched up tightly in her corset and sheathed in a crimson ball gown. She imagined Calvin had wearied of her melancholy and wished her to move on from her infatuation with Sheriff Garrison. He tried not to belittle her emotions, but it was obvious he was confident that the sheriff did not share her feelings.

A gentleman stepped up and bowed. "May I have this dance?"

Dread took hold and before she could stop herself, she turned and ran from the room. In her haste, she tripped over her own two feet and fell, her crinoline flipped up with revealing her chemise. Humiliated, she pushed her clothing down and held it in place, as she tried to regain her footing. The same gentleman who'd asked her to dance reached a hand out to assist her. Her face burned with embarrassment. She took the proffered hand and stood with great difficulty.

"My apologies, Madame. I hadn't meant to startle you. I only wished to offer a dance. I thought you might appreciate the company. Please excuse my forwardness."

"No. I am the one who should apologize. I have not attended many of these events and am not in the habit of dancing. I startled too easily."

"Shall we try again?"

She nodded.

"May I have this dance?"

"Yes, thank you." She allowed herself to be swept away in the man's arms. She didn't even know his name and at this moment as he held her for the waltz, she imagined what it would be like to dance with Jack in such a way. Blinking away a tear, she forced herself back into the moment.

Halfway through the dance, another man tapped her dance partner on the shoulder "May I cut in?" The sound of Jack's voice startled her.

It couldn't be him. She met his gaze and nearly melted into the floor. "Jack?"

"Yes, Miss Belle, it is I." The other man backed off, and Jack gathered her in his arms.

"What are you doing here at a ball in Philadelphia?" She drank in his pleasant, slightly leathery scent as he leaned close.

"Would I miss the opportunity to support this reputable charity?"

"You do not know what the charity is, do you?"

"No."

"Then why are you here?"

"Calvin and Sarah said you would be here."

She couldn't believe what she was hearing. He'd come for her. "Did you seek me for a reason?"

"Yes, but I would prefer to discuss the reason after the ball."

When the music stopped, he got her a glass of punch and stood silently beside her while she drank.

"It is a shock to see you, sheriff."

"Is it?" He grinned.

She nodded. "The New Mexico Territory is a great distance from Philadelphia. I thought to never see you again."

"That would have been a sad state of affairs."

"How so?" She raised an eyebrow.

"They are playing a polka. Do you know it?"

"Calvin made sure I learned the standard dances whether I chose to or not."

"Would you care to dance with me?"

Grace longed for him to explain why he was there. She hoped to hear that he'd come this far to fetch her. Had he fallen in love with her the way she had him? She shouldn't allow herself such whimsical fantasies. As he steered her onto the floor, her remaining questions went unasked, and speech became impossible as he spun her around the dance floor.

When the song ended he led her away again. She allowed herself the luxury of standing too close to him regardless of propriety. It might be their last night together, so she would make the memories count. Whatever he'd come for, she was sure he wouldn't be in town for a prolonged stay. He loved Cimarron too much to remain away.

He brushed the hair from her neck and whispered in her ear. "You look stunningly beautiful tonight, Grace."

She felt another blush warm her cheeks. "Thank you."

"Do I embarrass you?"

"No."

"Then why are you blushing?"

She lowered her lids to look away from his intense stare. He gently pushed her chin up, so she was once again looking into his eyes. "I blush easily."

"Maybe." He put his hand on the small of her back and steered her toward the coat closet. "I know it's a cold winter night, but I wondered if you would consider a walk with me?"

She shivered at the thought, but not from the cold. Calvin wouldn't approve of her leaving the charity auction to consort with a man, but at that moment, she didn't care. She intended to savor those last few moments with the man who'd stolen her heart.

Jack maneuvered Grace toward the exit. The fragrance of honeysuckle surrounding her affected him. He needed to get her alone.

Even in the enormous ballroom, the crowd felt stifling. He lived in New York for a few years when his father had sent him back east to attend school. It wasn't his preference, but he could live in a big city if need be. He would make the sacrifice for Grace.

He helped her into her coat and led her toward the waterfront. Voices singing *O Holy Night* floated on the air. "Do you hear that?" He got chills as he listened to the words, and his heart was filled to overflowing with a deep love for Christ.

"Yes, it's a beautiful hymn."

He took her by the hand and stopped walking. "It must be carolers. We don't get much of that in the territories."

"Imagine that." She giggled.

"Do you want to listen a while?"

She nodded. Snow flurries swirled around them sticking to her eye lashes. The intense emotion in her trusting green eyes mesmerized him. He wondered again if she would have him as her husband, or if she would send him away.

When the song ended they continued to walk until he found a spot along the riverfront that offered them a modicum of privacy. A hearty breeze swirled Grace's dress around her reminding him of earlier. "I witnessed your mishap when I entered the ballroom."

"Now I am mortified."

"I thought it was sweet."

"What was sweet about it?"

He pulled her close and breathed the words into her ear. "You were running from another man."

She smiled demurely. "Was I?"

"You certainly were." He could read the truth in her eyes. Reaching out, he caressed her cheekbone with the back of his fingers before trailing the edge of his index finger along her throat. He felt the pulse at the base of her neck with his thumb. Reaching up he removed the pins from her hair and let the silky strands fall, running them between his fingers. They were as soft as he expected. He pulled her closer to him and let his hands rest on either side of her tiny waist. "Grace, I am not in Philadelphia by chance."

"Why are you here, Jack?"

"To ask you to be my wife." He lowered his head to hers, and gently brushed her lips with his. The kiss started out sweet, but quickly increased in urgency. His heart swelled with love for her.

When he finally broke off the kiss, she met his gaze. "Why would you ask me such a thing?" Grace took his hands in hers and held them close to her heart. "You told me I belong in Philadelphia not with you in the territories."

"You do."

"You are not making sense."

"I am asking if you will have me as your husband. I will leave my home in Cimarron and stay here with you."

"You love your home. The people. The landscape. Your father is close. Everything about it appeals to you."

"Your brother is here."

"He can afford to come visit."

"This city is all you've ever known. You have conveniences here that we won't have in Cimarron in our lifetimes. How could I ask you to leave your home?" he asked.

"I would have stayed with you."

"I know."

"Then why did you let me leave?"

"I nearly didn't." He sighed. "It wounded me deeply to watch that train pull away before I told you how I felt."

"How do you feel?"

"I love you, Grace. I want you to be my wife."

"I love you too, but I won't marry you if it means you will stay here."

"You won't marry me?"

"That is not what I said."

"Yes, you did."

"I *will* marry you. I want to marry you, but only if we go back to the New Mexico Territory. It's where you belong. You could never be happy here."

"You belong here."

"I belong beside you. Wherever you are."

"You would give up everything for me?"

"Yes, but may we get chickens and a cow? The fresh eggs at the Rutherfords were delicious, and I always wanted to try milking a cow."

"Are you serious with this now?"

"Yes. Well?"

"You can have whatever pleases you."

"In that case, I shall take you."

He lowered his head to hers and captured her lips in an urgent kiss.

Grace thought her heart would burst with the pent up emotions Jack was bringing to the surface. The touch of his lips on hers brought every nerve ending in her body to life. She needed this man and he'd come all this way for her. When he set her away from him, she felt the loss.

"I'm having difficulty keeping control, Grace." He took her hand and started walking back toward the hotel hosting the ball.

The cool breeze off the Delaware River ruffled her hair reminding her that she was disheveled, with her hair hanging loosely down her back. "How soon can we get married?"

"If there's a preacher available, tonight is acceptable." He slid his arm around her waist and pulled her into his side as they walked.

She couldn't stop grinning. This man would soon be her husband. "Tomorrow will be soon enough."

"Do you not desire a formal affair with many guests?"

"Provided that you and I are there in the presence of God, I need no other witnesses." She slowed her steps.

The words seemed to please him, as he stopped walking and drew her into his arms once again. He gently brushed his lips against hers in a teasing kiss, before deepening the kiss and groaning against her mouth. "We need to stop this, but we can pick up where we left off on our wedding night."

"You are making me wish our wedding was this night."

"Me too." He laced his fingers with hers and walked them back toward the ball.

"I cannot go back inside looking like this?"

"You are beautiful."

"Thank you, but I am disheveled. People will talk. They will conclude that we did more than steal a few kisses."

"Let them talk."

"My brother has a reputation to uphold and I would not wish to destroy his good name by embarrassing him at his charity event. Is it okay if we head back to the manor?"

"It would be a delight to dance the night away with you, Grace." He reached for her hair. "I messed up your hair, so I will fix it." The touch of his fingers against her neck sent jolts of pleasure dancing along her skin.

"Ever the gentleman." She had no idea how well he'd repinned her hair, but decided to trust him.

They danced through nearly every song.

As they strolled out to the carriage with Calvin and Sarah, the snow fell harder, covering everything. It was a beautiful sight to behold.

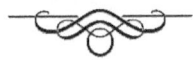

The four of them loaded into the carriage. When they'd settled into their seats, grace touched the other woman's elbow. "You look amazing, Sarah."

"So do you." Sarah grinned. "That ball gown is fabulous."

"Are you two finished complimenting each other?" Jack asked.

Grace giggled. "I suppose."

Jack leaned toward Calvin. "How soon can you get a preacher?"

"Depends on what you need the preacher for."

"So I can marry your sister."

"It will take time to plan a proper wedding, Jack."

"Grace doesn't want all the fancy trappings."

He looked to his sister. "Is this true?"

"It is." Grace reached over and squeezed Jack's hand. "I only want to become Jack's wife."

"Well, the preacher will be busy tomorrow being that it's a Sunday, but I could probably arrange for him to come over on Monday. Will a Christmas Eve wedding be satisfactory?"

"I couldn't choose a better day to be married. Is it acceptable to you, Grace?"

"Nothing would make me happier."

Joy filled Grace as she listened to the sounds of the city celebrating Christmas. Snow covered everything in a blanket of white. The magical beauty of the moment touched her, and she realized she had finally allowed Jesus unlock that cage around her heart, so that it could be filled with his peace. She was ready to celebrate His birth with her whole heart and soul.

Grace admired her fancy updo in the mirror. Sarah had dismissed the servants and styled Grace's hair herself. Slipping into her mother's wedding gown of ivory satin with emerald green trim, she turned to allow Sarah to button up the bodice. The dress had been the height of fashion when her mother wed in 1849. Grace spun around, luxuriating in the feel of the fabric floating around her.

"I was surprised you chose a late evening wedding, Grace."

"I think the lighting will be flattering, and it will allow us to celebrate Christmas after the wedding, since we are sure to be celebrating long after midnight."

"A wedding on the Eve of Christmas is an amazing way to celebrate the birth of Christ. I am sure we will all cherish the memory for years to come." Sarah stood back assessing her. "You're missing something."

"I am?"

"Earrings."

"Oh! My mother's emeralds would be amazing with this dress." She hurried off to get them, moving as quickly as her gown would allow.

"You make a beautiful bride, Grace."

"I am confident you will, as well. We'll come for the wedding if we are able."

"I hope you are able to attend," Sarah said.

"Will you wait a considerable length of time?"

"We're discussing a spring wedding in the courtyard."

"The flowers will be in bloom, it should be gorgeous," Grace said. "Will you stay here at the manor until then?"

"No. That wouldn't be proper. I found a place nearby."

"I wish we were making it a double wedding."

"Calvin and I will marry soon enough." Sarah wiped away a tear. "Your groom is waiting, shall we?"

Sarah proceeded her down the grand staircase and took her place. Grace slowly made her way down the stairs careful not to trip in her high-heeled boots. The sight of Jack waiting for her, brought fresh tears to her eyes.

Jack, dressed in a formal jacket, trousers and waistcoat, waited in opulent foyer, their few guests were seated and the preacher stood beside him. It amazed him how beautifully the wedding had come together.

The room had been decorated with pine sprigs and holly clippings, interspersed with white tulle and velvet ribbons. He took in the mild fragrance of pine mixed with candle wax. Candles had been lit in lieu of the fancy electric lighting recently added to the manor. He marveled again at Grace's willingness to give up her comforts to be with him.

He stared at the breathtaking vision in ivory satin glide down the stairs, a small train of silk following behind her. She seemed to float toward him and sight of her enchanted him. The minister began the ceremony, but Jack couldn't take his eyes off his bride.

With Grace's hands in his he spoke his vows. The love in her eyes was undeniable.

When she read her vows, he had to wipe away a tear. He was not a man given to emotional displays, but his bride touched something deep inside him igniting a passion he knew would not soon fade.

After they made their promises and the preacher pronounced them husband and wife, Jack lifted her into his arms and spun her around in a circle. He kissed her as if they were the only two people present.

Most of the night went by in a flurry of activity, but when the clock struck midnight, they all stood quietly, reflectively. After a minute of silence, someone began to sing *Silent Night* and they all joined in. The beauty of the holy night was complete as he tucked Grace close beside him and considered the sacrifice of Christ Jesus so many years before.

Epilogue

G race collected eggs and went inside to make a hearty breakfast. Having ridden through the night, Jack had arrived home from his trip to Santa Fe. He was washing away the dirt from his travels while she went about her morning chores. They had fresh meat from a butchered pig, so bacon was on the menu. It had taken time for her to learn how to cook without burning the biscuits at each meal, but with Mrs. Rutherford's patient assistance, she was making progress.

She stood at the cooker, frying the eggs, but backed away from the hot pan when Jack reached his strong arms around her waist.

"In another few months, you will not be able to fit your arms around me."

"I still can't believe Doc Murphy said there were two heartbeats."

"Neither can I." She wondered how she would keep up with two infants, but considering the love she felt for them already, she knew they would manage.

"I have a surprise."

"You do?"

"I bought another parcel of land. We will build a larger home."

"Really?" She grinned.

"My bride deserves a pleasant space to raise a family."

"I love you."

"As I do you." He lowered his lips to hers and she once again melted into his kiss, letting the eggs and bacon burn.

*I*saiah frowned as he scanned the telegram the ranch manager had brought from town. It looked like his Christmas vacation would be short-lived.

Thomas Hayes placed a hand on his shoulder. "What's wrong, son?"

"It's work. I've been summoned to investigate three hangings in McDade." Isaiah sighed. "I need to go there."

"Now? On Christmas day?"

"The townsfolk in McDade are known for taking justice into their own hands."

"I'm glad you could come home for Christmas." His father slapped him on the back. "Come back soon."

"I will." He hurried to his room and packed his meager belongings.

His brother, Nate, confronted him as he stepped into the hall. "In a hurry?"

"Unfortunately, yes."

"I'll ride with you to the Santa Fe station."

"It's your first Christmas with your wife. Stay with her. Send word when the baby comes, and I'll come back for a visit."

"I will." Nate gave him a quick hug. "Stay safe."

The ride to Santa Fe was uneventful and before he knew it, he was stepping off the train onto the platform in McDade, Texas. He picked up a horse at the livery and headed to see the acting sheriff.

The door of the McDade Sheriff's office swung open and John Olive grinned. "Glad to see your ugly mug, Ranger Hayes."

"I didn't expect to be back so soon."

"I wouldn't reckon you did."

"How is Sheriff Heffington's widow doing?"

"About as well as can be expected. It hasn't even been a month since his murder."

"Tell me about the hangings."

"Let's grab a bite at the saloon. There is quite a bit to tell. Matters got much worse after the hangings."

They headed to the saloon on foot, but a whinny got Isaiah's attention and he turned on his heel back toward the sheriff's office. A scruffy man was mounting his horse. Isaiah ran toward him, but before he could reach the man, he'd taken off at a gallop.

When Deputy Olive caught up to Isaiah, he was still bent at the waist with his hands on his knees catching his breath. "John, I'm going to need to borrow a horse."

Get your copy on Amazon:

https://www.amazon.com/Lawfully-Promised-Inspirational-Historical-Lawkeepers-ebook/dp/B07JQGP517/

Reader Letter

Dear Reader,

I hope you enjoyed reading my novel, *Lawfully Given*. Please check out some of my other titles.

I'd love it if you'd sign up for my newsletter at:
https://www.elleekay.com/newsletter-sign-up/.

If you enjoyed *Lawfully Given*, the most helpful thing you can do is leave an honest review. So, please consider submitting a review on Amazon and/or GoodReads. It doesn't cost anything other than a moment of your time and can be tremendously beneficial to me. Your quick review helps to get my book into the hands of other readers who may enjoy it.

https://www.amazon.com/Lawfully-Given-Inspirational-Historical-Lawkeepers-ebook/dp/B07J9VZND8/

https://www.goodreads.com/book/show/42305667-lawfully-given

For a list of my current books and upcoming releases check out the novel page on my website: https://www.elleekay.com/novels/

Thank you.
Elle E. Kay
https://www.elleekay.com

About Elle E. Kay

Elle E. Kay lives in the Back Mountain area of Pennsylvania. She loves life in the country on her little farmette. Elle is a born-again Christian with a deep faith and love for the Lord Jesus Christ. She desires to live for Him and to put Him first in everything she does.

She writes children's books under the name Ellie Mae Kay.

You can connect with Elle on her website and blog at https://www.elleekay.com/ or on social media:

Facebook: https://www.facebook.com/ElleEKay7

Twitter: https://twitter.com/ElleEKay7

Pinterest: https://www.pinterest.com/elleekay7/

Google+: https://plus.google.com/u/0/+ElleEKay

Amazon Author Central: http://www.amazon.com/author/ellekay

Instagram: https://www.instagram.com/elleekay7/

Goodreads: https://www.goodreads.com/author/show/15016833.Elle_E_Kay

I'd love it if you'd sign up for my newsletter at https://www.elleekay.com/newsletter-sign-up/

Acknowledgements

I would like to express my gratitude to my husband, Joe, for putting up with the long hours of writing and editing.

Any errors or deficiencies are my own.

Personal Testimony

I first came to know Jesus as a young teen, but before long I strayed from God and allowed my selfish desires to rule me. I sought after acceptance and love from my peers, not knowing that only God could fill my emptiness. My teen years were full of angst and misery, for me and my family. People I loved were hurt by my selfishness. My heartache was at times overwhelming, but I couldn't find the healing I desperately desired. After several runaway attempts my family was left with little choice, and they put me in a group home/residential facility where I would get the constant supervision I needed.

At that home I met a godly man called 'Big John' who tried once again to draw me back to Jesus. He would point out Matthew 11:28-30 and remind me that all I had to do to find peace was give my cares to Christ. I wanted to live a Christian life, but something kept pulling me away. The cycle continued well into adulthood. I would call out to God, but then I would turn away from Him. (If you read the old-testament you'll see that the nation of Israel had a similar pattern, they would call out to God and He would heal them and bring them back into their land. Then they would stray and He would chastise them. It was a cycle that went on and on).

When I came to realize that God's love was still available to me despite all my failings, I found peace and joy that have remained with me to do this day. It wasn't God who kept walking away. He'd placed his seal on me in childhood and no matter how far I ran from Him, **He remained faithful.** When I finally recognized His unfailing love, I was made free.

2 Timothy 2:13

"If we believe not, yet he abideth faithful: he cannot deny himself."

Ephesians 4:30

"And grieve not the holy Spirit of God, whereby ye are sealed unto the day of redemption."

I let myself be drawn into His loving arms and led by His precious nail-scarred hands. He has kept me securely at His side and taught me important life lessons. Jesus has given me back the freedom I had in Christ on that day when I accepted the precious gift He'd offered. My life in Him is so much fuller than it ever was when I tried to live by the world's standards.

I implore you, if you've known Jesus and strayed, call out to Him.

If you've never know Jesus Christ as your personal Lord and Saviour. Find out what it means to have a relationship with Christ. Not religion, but a personal relationship with a loving God.

God makes it clear in His word that there isn't a person righteous enough to get to heaven on their own.

Romans 3:10

"As it is written, There is none righteous, no, not one:"

We are all sinners.

Romans 3:23

For all have sinned, and come short of the glory of God;

Death is the penalty for sin.

Romans 6:23

"For the wages of sin is death; but the gift of God is eternal life through Jesus Christ our Lord."

Christ died on the cross for our sins.

Romans 5:8

"But God commendeth his love toward us, in that, while we were yet sinners, Christ died for us."

If we confess and believe we will be saved.

Romans 10:9

"That if thou shalt confess with thy mouth the Lord Jesus, and shalt believe in thine heart that God hath raised him from the dead, thou shalt be saved."

Once we believe he sets us free.

Romans 8:1

"There is therefore now no condemnation to them which are in Christ Jesus, who walk not after the flesh, but after the Spirit."

I hope you'll take hold of that freedom and start a personal relationship with Christ Jesus.